YOU COMPLETE ME

Claire Finneas

Contents

Part 1

A lexa

"Alexa! Table 3 now!" My manager said to me

Shit

I drift of to sleep he is gonna kill meee

My eyes shot open and i nodded hurriedly mouthing a 'sorry' with a sad face but he glared at me i look down

shutup you little dick man

Oh how do i know it ?Well everyone who work here said it he have small dick

I made my way towards table 3 smiling

"Hello sir and ma'am what would you guys like to have?" I ask in sweet voice

They gave their order and i noted it while nodding

"I'll bring your drinks first" i said smiling

"Cool" they said and i made my way towards the chef (george) one of my great friend

I told him all the order and he said it will be ready in 15 minutes He made the drinks quickly so i took it to the customers

And just like that my day goes well I don't what is gonna happen now that all the customers are gone and the restaurant is closed Its me and the manager JackHe hates me with every thing inside him

Although i have never done anything wrong I try my best to complete my target and make him happy but.... Anyways

"Bye Lexi" george said waving to me with a smile "Bye georgy" i said grinning

I cleaned the table and jack came towards me

"My office now" he said and i nodded looking down

I know what is gonna happen

God save me please

I walk inside his office and he was sitting he looked at me and smirked

Well just so you know he is in his 40-ish

"Well well Ms alexa" he said

"Yes sir" i muttered

"What will you like today?" He asked grinning

"Uh cup of coffee" i said blankly

He frowned "you know what i am asking"

I gulped

"I- i didn't do anything wrong today sir" my voice sad

He chuckled darkly "shut your mouth little bitch.. you drift to sleep 2 times and you made the customers wait"

"I will not do it again" i said looking at him with sorry eyes

"Well its too late" he said and my eyes widened he came towards me and stood infront of me

He grabbed my hair harshly pulling it i scream "s-sir it is hurting!"

"Well guess what i dont give a fuck" he said

He slapped me across the face really hard and it sting really hard

I shut my eyes tightly not wanting to cry

He said whenever i beat you don't cry or i'll beat you twice

He slapped me again there making it more stung i pressed my lips together with my eyes still shut

He pushed me back "get the fuck out and be on time tomorrow"

I looked down cause i know my eyes must be watering i nodded hurriedly

I took my purse and went out

My lower lip start trembling as it really hurts

I walk in my apartment opening the door and then i threw my purse away and shut the door sliding down crying my heart out

It took me good 15 minutes to get back to normal

I walked in bathroom and saw my face it was red and it had his finger prints

I use my face wash and it sting i hissed biting my lip i quickly washed my face

And then layed down on my bed changing in my comfy clothes

I turn the light off and get in bed then sleeping

Well this was my normal life

I am Alexa, as you all know i've been working in this cafe for 2 years since i ran from my house

I ran from my house because my father died and my mother became a drug addict she was in really bad state and i tried my best to recover her but i failed she just used to run away or sometimes bring any random guy and have sex with him I couldn't see it anymore so i ran away And then i met jackI wish i didn't but i did and he offered me a jobOne day being emotional i told him all my story and since then he have been taking advantage of it and i couldn't stop him as i need to live and to live we need to eat and to eat i should have money and to have money i have to work

Therefore

And he also let me rent an apartment

At first he used to pay the bill but now i do

This is my storyyy Boring i know *snorts*....

"Alexa you need to deliver this pizza" Jack informed me I was confused

"But i don't deliver" i said

"Delivery guy is not here bitch, and i'll give you 5 dollars extra now get out and deliver it address is in the slip

"I don't know how to drive" i mumble slowly

He groaned and threw the cab fare at my face

"Thankyou!!" I said smiling and walk out with pizza in my hand and me in my work outfit with a cap on

I took a cab and i told him address

We reached to a nice looking apartment and i licked my lips looking at it

I get inside the building walked towards the lift

....

Part 2

A lexa

The elevator opens and i step inside just as it was about to close i guy came in view

Oh my god this guy is so beyond handsomeI- What?He looks like a model

He had light brown hair which were styled back and his jawline hot as fudgeHis eyes grey oh i could watch it foreverAnd his big eyelashes, i am jealousHe was muscular (not a giant) but a hot muscular person

He was wearing black button down shirt top two buttons undone showing sneak peak of his hot chest following with black pants

How badly i wanna watch his naked chest

I think i am drooling

He blinked at me his face straight no emotionAnd he didn't asked me to stop it but i did Me being me

He step inside looking at me for second then his back on me

what cologne is he wearing??Oh my god my mouth is wateringIt felt like an expensive cologne Obviously Alexa!!

I almost moaned

Oh god i shook my head and looked at him

Well hello mister 'Handsome Hot Nugget' no thankyou ?

He pressed 20th floor Oh that is my floor too!I grinned

"I am also going on that floor" i said smiling

He couldn't see me

He didn't answered nor he turned around

I clear my throat "i said i am also going on that floor!" I said now stepping beside him i could see his gorgeous face

He didn't answered again

My eyebrows scrunch together

"Uh do you speak?" I ask

His face serious but now a little irritated

"Helloo?? Pink panther??" I said

His head towards me and he glared at me

"Oh you can listen" i sighed "thankyou!"

I chuckled "what would i do if you didn't?"

He frowns at me

"You know i speak a lot like a lot and i can go on and on" i said proudly

He gave me a 'seriously?' Look Which means not interested

He looked at the elevator door again ignoring me

"What is your name by the way? My name is alexa you can call me lexi" I said shrugging

No reply....

"Uhh let me guess" i hummed thinking

"Chimpanzee? Orrr horse face orr hmm yeah! Pink panther?" I asked grinning at him with excitement

I criss cross my fingers praying May one of it be his name

He looked at me glaring the hell outta me

I pursued my lips "okayy sorryy uh" i stopped so he could say his name

I raise my eyebrows He lightly shrugged now taking his eyes of my face

"Well okay i'll go with chimpanzee" i smile sweetly at him

"Do you have a fucking switch button?" He asked in his sexxxyyy voice

oh lala

"Why would i carry a switch button with me?" I ask tilting my head lightly "do i have to?" I bit my lip thinking

He pinched the bridge of his nose closing his eyes The corner of his lips turn up lightly in annoyance

I saw and the elevator was on 18

I nodded to myself

The elevator shake and my eyes widened while that guy tense

It stopped ShitShit

My eyes widened with fear and pizza box fell of my hand

I screamed "Shutup!" That guy said louder

I stopped and looked at him "We are gonna die! Chimpanzee!" I said fear in my eyes

He rolled his eyes and leaned back crossing his arm "first of all we are not gonna die shut the fuck up and second of all cut your bullshit by calling me chimpanzee"

Wow he said it all at once?

I bit my lip trying my best not to laughAnd nodded he narrowed his eyes

"Why did the elevator got stucked!!" I said biting my lip

I looked at him and saw him looking down at my lip i blushed a little he looked away

He pressed emergency button and then called someone on his phone"What the fuck is wrong with your apartment's elevator" he asked someone on the phone while frowningGosh he looks so cutee

He shake his head to something the guy said on phone and some strand of his hair falls on his forehead making him look more cuter like a cat, meow"Fuck off" he said and hung up slipping his phone in the back pocket

"I need to deliver this pizza it will turn cold" i said to him when he looked at the pizza

He looked me in the eye without glaringWoah

"You know i work at this restaurant and it is really nice it is i guess 5 minutes from here and oh! I am not the rider" i chuckled "i am the waitress and you know the guy i work with is so nice i mean he is my great friend and his name is george, he is a nice guy sometimes i even think he has a crush on me! By the way he looks at me but no then there is my manager a really idiot and stupid person i've ever met but i couldn't do anything ya know and i like to eat donuts a lot! It is like my fav thing whenever i am sad or whenever i need a hug i eat my donut and... Oh! have you eaten strawberry donut-" he cuts me off

"Breathe" he said

My eyebrows scrunch together

"You need to breathe" he complete his sentence shoving his hands in his pocket

"Oh do i have to?" I ask him i gasp dramatically "i totally forgot that thankyou!! I would've died good god!" I said

He rolled his eyes glaring at me

I bit my lip giggling "sorry"

"Do you live here?" I asked him

Silence

"Anyways.. will you go eat donut with me after i am done with my shift?" I ask my eyes widening with excitement

"Your donut and you can go fuck yourself" he said bitterly

My low lip tremble as i try my best not to cry

"okay" i mumble and look down

guess i will not talk

I tried my really best and stayed quiet then after some time our elevator was repaired

"It was nice meeting-" he walked away

strange man

I shrugged to myself and walked towards the apartment number

I ring the bell and an old lady came to open the door Suddenly my heart melted

I smiled at her brightly "Hi!"

She smiled at me "hello honey"

"You ordered your pizza, here you go! I am so sorry i am late your apartment's elevator got stuck" i said nodding to myself

She shook her head still smiling her wrinkles look so beautiful on herShe is a beautiful woman "it is okay dear"

"You can come inside" she offers

"That is so sweet of you! I'll come next time! I have to work now sorry" i said feeling sorry

"No it is okay, you can come whenever you want afterall i live by myself" she said

And i felt my heart getting heavy...My smile dropped

"What is your name dear?" She asked

"A-alexa" i stutter

"Beautiful name" she said and i smiled

"Can i call you grandma? I dont have one" i said

"Ofcourse! I would love that!" She said happily making my heart happy

"Okay grandma! Gotta go now bye enjoy your pizza" i kissed her cheek

"But money-" i cut her

"No no, my treat" i said and she hugged me saying thankyou

She was really sweet

This time i took the stairs and left the building going to the cafe/restaurant whatever

Just as i entered cafe/restaurant whatever i saw angry jack

Shit..

...

He beat me today also but with his belt this time on my back he hurt 5 times and it hurt

I went to get medical kit but thought of showing it to doctorShe was shocked i told her i fell from stairs

She nodded but her eyes showed it completely that she caught my lie but didn't talked about it. Good. I don't want to

I walk out of the doctor's room and walked towards the elevator just as i saw

Chimpanzee?

...

Sorry for the cliffhanger!! Next chapter will be up soon□

Part 3

Guys don't forget to VOTE please

Alexa

His arm was bandaged Oh god

Chimpanzee got in a fight with gorilla?

I walk up to him "oh god, what happened?" I asked him

He was sitting on a chair his head was leaned back and his eyes were closed but it open when he heard meHe frowns "what are you doing here?" He asked

"Hey! Don't steal my words" i said

"I had an small accident" he said leaning his head back again closing his eyes

"Small? Seriously, it looks like you have bad accident!" I said my eyes widening"Does it hurt?" I asked softly pouting a little

I cant feel him Poor boy must've hurt alot

His eyes open and he looked at me his head still leaning back"No" he said harshly "why are you here?" He asked his eyes narrowing

"Oh i- i yes! I came here to see a friend" i said smiling

He didn't answered but his eyes narrowed alittle more i looked away not meeting his gaze

"Bro it hurt like motherfucker" some guy came up to him and said holding his head

Oh shit His head is bandaged His age looks similar to chimpanzee

"Oh my god! Are you fine?" I asked that guy

His eyes flickered to me "who must be you pretty girl?" He aksed smiling

I blushed alittle

I was about to answer when chimpanzee spoke "you don't need to know, she talks alot"

"I don't mind that" he grinned at chimpanzee while he glared at him and i dont know what happened he nodded

"I am gonna be in car, come" that guy said and left smiling at me i returned it

I turned towards him "what was that chimpanzee?"

"What?" He asked like he doesn't know anything "stop calling me that" he scrunched his noseCute as fudge

I sighed "that guy, who was he? and he was being nice and you wouldn't let me talk to him and i do not talk alot! And i will call you chimpanzee because i don't know your name so i didn't have any choice but to call you that and also-" he cuts me

"Shut up!" He said louder i flinch a little

"You don't wanna know him and me" he said glaring at me

"Oh come on! You wouldn't eat a donut with me?" I pouted "but you said you would" i pouted again

He never said that

His eyes went down to my lips and it came back to my eye "I never said that" he said

I nodded my head confidently "yes you did! I remember nicely" i told him proudly

"I must be drunk or whatever" he said rolling his eyes

"Please??" I pouted giving him puppy eyes

"Do better"

I groan "Fine! Don't come with me to eat my favourite strawberry donut with cold ice latte. Fine" i said to him

Silence

I clear my throat and he was still looking at me not glaring, looking

"What?" I ask folding my arms and rolling my eyes dramatically

"What is your friend's room number i wanna meet him too" he said now standing

My eyes widening a little "uh i- he was discharged!" I said smiling

He tilt his head "i didn't see him coming out"

I gulped

"What are you hiding?" He asked glaring at me

I groaned "0kay fine!! I fell from the stairs" i stick my tongue out to him after telling this

He scrunch his nose then his face still "i don't see any bandages"

I roll my eyes "its in the back dumb head"

He stepped towards me making my eyes widening a little "dumbhead?" He ask in his low voice

Well yes Hot nugget yesss

I gulp and shake my head "i said it to myself"

He didn't say anything

"Please tell me your name orr go with me to eat donut?" I said making puppy eyes

"Harry" he said

Harrrrryyyyyy

"Why do u hate my donut so much?" I ask groaning "well okay anyways, bye harry"

"Where are you going?" He asked walking with me

"Home, sweet home" i said nodding

"Its not safe at this time i'll drop you" he said

"That is really sweet of you but-" he cuts me off

"I was not asking" he said and walked faster

"Well hello gorilla size man, walk slow!!" I said

He didn't answered nor he walked slow

...

I got inside his car and and that guy was sitting in driver's seat while harry sat in passenger seat and me in backseat

His car was luxurious, i didn't know the name but it is WOW

"Helloo again beautiful" that guy said grinning

"Hii!" I said smiling brightly

"What is your name?" I asked him

"Logan" he said

"Mine is alexa you can call me-" harry cuts me off

Urghhh

"Alexa" he replied

I frowned

"Can you tell me your address?" Logan asked

"Uh yeah! Sure, its not like i will go at your home" i said chuckling awkwardly

"Do you want to?" He asked grinning

"Shut the fuck up logan before i smack your head in this steering wheel" harry said

Woah grumpy

I told him my address and me and logan chatted a little then harry said 'shut up"

He drove through the familiar streets and i looked out of window and then i saw donuts shop

It was closed...

I sighed

After some time

"Stop stop just right here" i said he stopped the car

"Well there ya go" logan said smiling

"Thankyou so much logan! It-"

Harry clears his throat

"Oh. sorry, thankyouuu so much harry" i said smiling

He looked back at me then rolled his eyes "fuck off now"

"Okay!" I said grinning

I step out of car and fell

What in the mother world

I heard door open and close

I groaned touching my knee "oh god" i muttered to myself boringly

I just came back from the hospital!

I saw large hands wrap around my waist and it helped me up

I turned around and those grey eyes were glaring at me "can't you be careful?" He asks

"S-sorry i just fall" i said

His hands were still around my waist and it was weird kind of warmth that it brought to my body

"I can go now" i said

He rolled his eyes and his hands on the small of my back he lead me to my apartment

I turned around i smiled "you are so sweet harry" i said

And kissed him on the cheek he froze

"On the other cheek also?" I asked him

No answer

Okay then.

I step on my tip toes i kissed his another cheek softly

I backed off smiling "bye bye!"

He didn't say anything and went away

..

I went inside my room and threw myself on the bed sighing

I closed my eyes and saw those grey eyes

Today he was behaving a little different, why ?

I shrugged to myself

I wish i could kiss those lips

What the-

What kind of weird desires are coming in my mind

Its strange

I shook my thoughts away

And slept dreaming of me eating the huge donut in the world i smile in the
dream then i saw harry over there eating with me Huh?

....

I try my best to not disappoint y'all i hope you guys appreciate my work!
It will mean alot to me!! I love you all so much you have no idea☐

Part 4

A lexa

"I am going for a lil bit of shopping ya know" i said to george while i was cleaning the table

Jack had a fever today so he gave us off early so i thought why not lets just go for shopping

"That is nice" he replied removing his gloves

"Yeah so will you like to join? We'll eat donuts" i said wiggling my eyebrows

He chuckled "sure"

"Cool"

"I'll pick you up" he said

I shrugged "okay"

...

Georgy picked me up and we went to the mall

He said dinner was on him i tried to say no

Keyword: tried

Anyhow we are still in the mall as i look for the top i saw last month i decided to buy it but its not here

"What are you looking for lexi" george asked roaming here and there cause clearly telling me he is bored but when i asked him that donkeyface said no i am enjoying it

"Uh i saw some top last month and i liked it a lot but its not here i think that collection is ended maybe"

He nodded "okay now shall we head to cash counter?"

"Yeah yeah lets go" i said

I held his hand and he was shocked but didn't said no

Well when someone is close to me i show them my love by holding their hands,arms actually being touchy touchy

There was a huge line at the cash counter

Took us some time

After fighting for 5 minutes i paid Thankgod

We went to some nice cafe

"Yes table for two" george replied to the manager he nodded and asked us to follow him

We sat across each other

It was 8:pm

We ordered for ourselves and then we started chatting

George start talking about his family and how much he loves his little sister

I gotta tell you boy he is handsome He have blue eyes and he is not muscular but still is cute and handsome (not more than harry)

I listen to him intently while he talks so lovingly about his sister

I smile at him when he laughs at something his little sister did when she was younger

George stopped talking and looked behind me his eyebrows scrunching

"What happened?" I ask him

"I don't know there is some weird guy at the back who is glaring at me for no reason and showing me his middle finger" he said

I was angry I turned around ready to kill him by my glare but instead my eyes pop out of the socket

Wait What??

The man there standing was none other than harry, he was wearing grey formals today first two buttons undone while one of his hands in the pocket and his hair a hot mess looking sexxyyyyyHe was glaring at george his nose flared

Oh do i forgot to tell you how fudging hot he look

His eyes flicked to me and he didn't glared for some second but then he glared me too

Arghhhh seriously??

I turned around ignoring him

"Do you know him?" George asked looking at my back for a second then at me

"Huh? Me?" I asked biting my lip

"No your donut" george said sarcastically

"Well my donut may know him but i don't" i shook my head "nuh uh never seen his handsome face before"

He nodded slowly

Harry was now infront of us looking down at george still glaring at him

"Harry" i called him

"wait you-" i cut george off

"George wait a second i'll be back" i said to him

"You sure will you be safe-" harry cut him off

"Shut the fuck up"

"Harry, behave" i said

He rolled his eyes

I nodded at george that i will be fine reassuring him I walked out of the cafe with harry following me behind

I went towards the empty street beside the cafe Then i turned around folding my arms

"What?" I asked him

"Who was that?" He asked his jaw clenched

Holy-

Not now alexa not now

"Why do you wanna know? You don't even like my donut" i said tilting my head

He stayed quiet just looking at my face no hint of emotion on his face

"You're beautiful" he muttered

My cheeks turned pink and i look down blushing

Did he really??

"T-thankyou" i mumbled pushing a strand of my hair behind my ear

"He was my friend from work, george and he is just a friend thats it" i told him

He came towards me and i step back then my back hit the wall

"h-harry" i whispered my throat dry

He was extremely close to me and his cologne was making me want to jump on him and bite him, hehe

"We are really close" i said softly

"I am aware" he whispered

Then he snaked his arms on my waist making me i froze then he burried his face in my neck

A bunch of butterflies came in my stomach

This feeling is really weird

I slowly hugged him back

I put my chin on his shoulder while caressing his back slowly

"I gotta go harry" i said to him softly

"1 min" he mumbled in my neck

"Harry-" he cut me off

"5 second"

I sighed closing my eyes and enjoying the moment

I wish this moment could freeze and i could stay like this forever

Then finally he backed off I looked in his grey eyes I think i fell in love with those eyes

"When did you came here?" I asked him

"Need to handle a business, since 1 hour" he shrugged

"I didn't saw you" i said

"I did" he said then his jaw clenched "with him"

"What is wrong with him being with me" i said folding my arms

"Everything" he replied i sighed

I walked inside then i saw harry was following me i frowned but didn't say anything

"I am sorry i am late" i said to george feeling sorry The food was here and he wasn't eating

He shook his head "its okay" he smiled

I sat across him then harry came and sat beside me leaning back in his chair looking at george more like glaring

"Why is he here" george said to me

"Gotta problem?" Harry asked his jaw clenching

"George just leave him think like he's not here okay? Lets talk" i told him and then i saw harry looking at me frowningI'll kiss you if you don't stop being cute

I ignored him and then i tried talking to george

Harry didn't let george talk so we didn't talk but ate in silence

I looked at harry and saw him looking at me

Mann are you in love with me?

I made a bite and pushed it infront of his mouth he shook his head but i glared at him daring him to say no He ate chewing slowly i smiled Good boy

I think harry liked it because he opened his mouth again so i fed him and ate myself while george was looking at us awkwardly

Nevermind (he would say that)

While i was feeding harry he had a little sauce at the corner of his lips so i extend my hand and wiped it off

I made eye contact with him and he was looking at me like i am the only person here

I looked away strange feeling in my stomach came back and it only comes when i am around him

Harry and george argued over who would pay the bill and harry won

"So now your favourite donut now?" George asked smiling when we got up

I nodded smiling widely

"You may fuck off now" harry said shoving his hands in the pocket still glaring at him

Poor boy

"Harry" i warned him

Then i looked at george who was looking in deep thought, maybe he is thinking what he did wrong to harry

"Yeah sure george lets go!" I said grinning george snap out of his thoughts

"Cool i'll be outside" he said and left

I started walking just when

Harry's warm hand grabbed my hand pulling me back "you are not going with him"

SorryI didn't heard ya

"I am" i said in a 'shut the hell up' tone

He narrowed his eyes "no"

"yes"

He shook his head "nope"

"yessss"

"No-" i cut him off by pecking his lips his eyes widened and my also eyes widened

What did i-

Did i really- Shit-

"I-" i was out of words and so was he

We just looked at each other shocked

"F-forget it happened" i muttered

He nodded licking his lips

Huh

"I- i think i am not gonna go with him" i said fiddling with my fingers

"I'll go with you" he mumbled

My head snapped up at him my eyes widened with excitement "really!?" I said grinning

He rolled his eyes "yes"

I jumped up and down grinning and while he looked at me his eyes and feature were softened

I grabbed his hands "lets go then!"

I lead him outside hella excited

There was george standing talking to someone on phone he hung up and turned towards me

"Hey uh george mind if-" harry cut me off

"Mind if you go fuck yourself" harry said fake smiling at him

Oh god Even if he fake smiled but good god his smile was sooo cuteeee Why don't he smile often??

We were still holding hands

"Do i know you? Or did i ever do anything to you?" George asked curiously

"Harry" i glared at him "shut up" i said

He gave me a boring look

I turned towards george "ignore him, so i think what if we catch up for donut next time? Sounds good?" I ask him smiling a little

He nodded "yeah, sure no problem"

"Great!" I said and went towards him

I hugged him while harry came and grabbed my arms softly pushing me away from him i frown at him

"Enough of hugging" he said looking at george

George said bye to me and left

Harry turned towards me "don't be touchy with him, or anyone" he said frowning

I narrowed my eyes "why? Look when someone is close to me i like expressing my love like this" i told him

"Do you like him?" He ask in low voice

You.

"What? No!" I said looking at him like he's mad

"don't do it next time not with anyone, you don't know what the dickheads are thinking of doing to you" he said his expression became angry thinking of that

Don't you also think that?I shook my thoughts

"They don't think like that harry" i said in boring tone

"Only if you knew" he muttered

"Okayy! I won't, now lets go i want my donut" i said licking my lips of thinking of donut harry's eyes went down to my lips and he gulped i blushed

I started walking and this time I didn't hold his hand

I am gonna make him taste his medicineDoes this fit here?

...

Harry drove the car while i was in passenger seat There was no music playing Boringgg

But not boring at the same time cause i know he is beside me so i feel good, great actually

I looked out of window thinking about the little kiss we shared or should i say i shared because it was only me who kissed himAnd well it was really fast but he still could've kissed back

His lips were really soft i swear

I mean if you kissed him

Don't even try

So you will feel how soft his lips are and you would never want to stop kissing him

I felt him pulling over then i looked at him

"Where are we?" I asked looking outside the window

"You wanted donut" he answered while unbuckling his seatbelt

"But-"

"Lets go" he said and i step out of the car

He brought me to a really nice cafe and i bet it would be really expensive just by looking at it

Soft music playing when we walked inside i was walking behind harry

"Mr Stewart!" Manager approached us He looked in his late 30s "great to have you here" while harry nodded

"I'll show you your table sir follow me" he said and we followed him

He took us to Vip section, huh?

They have vip section in the cafe

There was comfortable expensive sofa laying there following with an expensive and gorgeous table There was a glass window showing outside view

"I would sent the waiter right away sir, here is the menu i'll let you guys decide" the manager said

"Thankyou so much!" I said smiling at himHe returned it

"Okay hold up, do you have a super power?" I ask him narrowing my eyes he scrunch his nose "please tell me you do! I have some wishes would you fulfil them? If you do i would give you a huge hug with uh..." i count on my fingers "yeah! 10 kisses on each cheek" i said grinning

"I wish i had" he mumbled in his breath

I didn't heard him clearly

"Sorry?" I said

"Nothing and i don't have any super powers stop talking and order" he pushed menu infront of me

The waiter came shortly and i ordered

" i am gonna have uh" i think while tapping a finger on my lips "Spanish latte with 3 donuts! 2 Strawberry 1 chocolate"

He nodded and looked at harry he just shook his head and then the waiter left saying he'll bring it shortly

"Don't judge me that i eat that much" i said in one breathe

He scrunch his eyebrows in confusion "why would i?"

"Well mostly people do" i said biting my lip

"They are just fools" he said rolling his eyes

And i am a fool for you..

Fudgeee am i falling for him??

....

This chapter was really long! HahaI hope you enjoyed it And i hope you enjoyed harry being jealous and possessive ;) cause i enjoy a lot writing those scenes

More scenes like these will be coming!□

I Love you all!

Part 5

Harry

What the fuck is she doing with my brain

When i look at her all of my problems seem to go away

She have a weird addiction with donut and that she talks alot but i don't have any problem with that

I watch her as she look at her donut like its the love of her life

She take a bite and moan and my pants tighten

What the fuck

I clear my throat and adjust myself in the seat i think she got a sign because her cheeks turn pink

"Do you want one?" She asks her mouth full as she chew her donut

I shook my head with a little smile

"Oh okay" she said and shrugged

Then her head snapped up to me i raise an eyebrow Her eyes widened "did you smiled!?" She said gasping

"Huh?" I said

"You smiled didn't you?" She said grinning

"I-" this is the first time in my life when i stutter

"Caught ya!!" She said and giggled while she got up and shocked me

She hugged me

That is the best thing that she does to me

I hugged her back sighing and closing my eyes

"Umm harry?" She said

I hummed in response

"Can you leave me? My donut is waiting"

I rolled my eyes and let her go

She smiled awkwardly and started eating her donut

While i watch her, the light freckles she have on her nose, her dark brown wavy hair her gorgeous plump lips that i wanna kiss, she kissed me today while we were arguing and that was the best way to shut me upHer lips tasted like strawberry,

"You know donut is the only best thing happened to me in this life, ohh it tastes like heaven" she said her mouth still full as she talk

"Don't talk when you're eating" i said

She mimics me and i narrow my eyes at her

But i find it cute

"You should eat it" she suggested again

"No i-" i was cut off when she shoved a bite in my mouth

I scrunch my nose at her "i said i didn't wanted to eat" i said it while my mouth was full

"Don't talk when you're eating" she said mimicking my deep voice throwing my words back at me

little -

She finished her donut and latte then i payed for it she said she will pay but when she saw bill she passed it back to me awkwardly

"Harry the donut shop near my house is wayyy affordable than this" she said wiping her mouth with a tissue

"I know" i said typing away on my phone then i shoved it in my pocket

"You know i brought you here just so you could eat with me" she sighed "ohh yeaa! You must be out of money" she hummed at herself

I chuckled "no darling"

"You weren't?" She asked

"Not even a little close" i said smirking a little

I make alot of money through my company and because of my hardwork i deserve itIts in billions

She gasped "oh boy"

...

Alexa

"Are you serious?" I ask him if he's joking my eyes widened

He smirked and boy do he look hot

"Why would i lie lex?" He said tilting his head a little

Lexx

I don't know why but i blushed a little

"Whatever" i mumbled and he still had that sexy smirk

...

he dropped me off after this and i thanked him

And harry being harry No replyJust a simple look he gave me and then he drove away

I open the lights of my room and saw it was not as maintained as it is because today i was in a hurry so i left without keeping the things at their place

I sighed and dropped my bag at the chair and start cleaning my room

After 15 minutes my room was cleaned i dust off my hand and release a breathe

After that i climbed into shower and washed myself off singing 'the way i are' Like i was the famous singer and its my concert

After my concert

I changed into my shorts and tank top

then i laid down on my bed closing my eyes and smiling

Then i heard

Oops i did it againI played with your heartGet lost in the game Oh baby baby

I furrow my eyebrows when my eyes are shut

Then my eyes flicked open

I pick up my phone

Unknown number

Who the hell is calling me at this time!

I pick it up

"Hello?" I said

"Lex"

I frown

Harry?

"Harry? Is it you?" I sit up

"yeah"

I push one strand of my hair back my ear

"Is everything okay? Are you fine? Don't tell me you get into an accident again i swear harry, how the hell can one person be so careless-" he cuts me off

"Oh for fuck sake shutup now, listen to me"

I sighed "i am listening"

"I can't go home today, there is some work going on over there so all the ways leading to my home is closed.. i have got other apartments in other countries but can't go there at this time"

"That is.... weird" i said rubbing my right eye "you can come to my house for today" i said yawning

"Can i?"

I groan "yeah don't be formal now come" i said

"Okay" he hung up

Man he drives too fast Cause he reached here in less then 5 minutesAlthough one time i asked him how much far his house is from mine he said around 20 minutes but he drives fast so it doesn't take long

I open the door revealing harryHe was still in his work clothes looking *coughs* lets leave it

I moved out of my way and let him come in

He came inside taking his shoes off i smiled at him

he sat on the sofa in the lounge

My house is not really nice but i have decorated it nicely and with affordable stuff

There lays a small light grey sofa set and there is a small plant at the side following with a tv infront of the sofa there is a grey carpet on the floor

And I took a loan to buy a tv and sofa

..

He leans back sighing and then remove his suit jacketthen fold his sleeves up

Boy have some mercy

His hands oh my god His veins flex when he roll his sleeves upHe lose his tie

He looks like he is married to me and he came back from work and i was waiting for my cute hot husband

I shook my thoughts away

"Harry what are you doing?" I ask

He looks at me "am i not suppose to get comfortable?"

I chuckle "ofcourse, but why here?" I ask folding my arms

He scrunch his nose "what are you trying to say"

I groan "i mean i have my room right there" i point at my room "duh, come on"

He didn't said anything and followed me

I closed my door when he came inside he sat on my bed looking comfortable

I sat beside him and yawned

"You should sleep, i'll lay down" he said

I nodded and laid down on my bed closing my eyes

I felt him take a pillow i open my eyes and saw he laid down on the floor

Man are you serious

I sit up "harry what are you doing"

"Sleeping?" It came out more like a question

"Are you gonna sleep on the floor?" I ask it like he has grown two heads

He scrunch his eyebrows "yeah"

I roll my eyes and pat on the side of my head "come on buddy there is a lot of space i am sure you can fit its not like you are hulk"

He narrow his eyes "don't call me buddy"

I snort "whatever"

I pushed myself inside so he could lay down

He stood up and start unbuttoning his shirt then he remove it and put it on the small sitting chair

I gulp looking at his body his toned chest his muscles his 8 packs!Holy cow-

I shut my eyes tightly

I felt a bed dip and he laid down

I open my one eye and looked at him his eyes were closed and he laid straight hands on his stomach

I moved a little closer and now our bodies were touching and he was bare chest

Jesus help me

He didn't made a move to be closer

I shut my eyes tightly and darkness took me

...

Part 6

- -

A lexa

This feels so good

I smile in my sleep as i snuggle closer to whatever the warm thingy it isDid i bought it?Something so worth the money?

I heard a heartbeat sound and i frowned in my sleep a littleA heartbeat? Huh

I open one of my eyes and saw i was laying totally, yea totally on harry my whole body crushing his body but he didn't seem disturbed or uncomfortable infact he looked comfortable

His long lashes came down to his high cheek bones, his lips a little parted as he sleep peacefully

How the hell do u look so hot while sleepingSomeone please kill me

Forgot to mention one of his hands was around my waist tightly and the other was laying beside him

And my arms were around his torso

I furrow my eyebrows Did something happened last night?I don't remember anything happening like this

I tilt my face and admired his face How can someone be so incredibly handsome it should be a sin

i removed my one hand from torso and cupped his cheek caressing it a little

'Have i started developing feelings for him'I thought to myself

'No it can't be'Another thought came to my mind

My eyes start feeling heavy again i checked the time and it was 6 in the morning I took my phone and saw jack has messaged me

I quickly opened it and saw 'The cafe will be off for today you guys don't have to come as i am not feeling really well'

I almost jump from excitement then i put it on my nightstand and untangled me from harry

And laid beside him but decided to cuddleSo i laid my head on his chest and felt my eyes heavy while listening to his soft breaths i fall asleep

..

I turned around and put an arm around the bed

Hmm?

No one is there

I opened my eyes and saw that the side where harry was laying no one was there

I sat up rubbing my eye i saw the time 12

Oh good heavens i slept for really long today

I got up from bed grabbed my phone and saw a message from unknown numberThe numner from which harry called

I saved it with 'nugget'

'Thanks for letting me stay, i had to leave because of some work purposes.. bye'

I read his message again and again smiling at myselftho it wasn't even romantic but stillThis sucker had me now

I changed into my comfy clothes and smiled looking at myself in the mirror

'What would it be like if me and harry were married and completely in love?'

Fake scenario of Alexa:

I stretch my arms as i release a breatheI look beside me harry sleeping his back on me, his back muscle looking hot

I smile at him faintly as i see him sleeping with no worriesHis lips slightly parted and his hair coming down on his forehead making him look soooo cuteee

I leaned in and pecked his lips softly

I get up but a strong hand wrap around my wrist pulling me down and i squeaked with surprise

I saw harry's eyes half open as he watch me with a little smile on his face

"Where do you think you are going baby?" He said in his deep voice but was more sexier in the morning

I smiled sheepishly "to eat my donut"

His smile went away and he looked bored

Then a smirk tug on his lips"Well your donut is here" he pointed at himself "so do the honours" he winked

And i blushed really hard "harry!"

He chuckled heavenly He leans in and kiss my forehead "You're gorgeous" he caressed my cheek and i leaned in his touch

"Harry i love the way you look at me" i whisper to him as my eyes closed

"Hm? Really?" He teases

I smiled and nodded "Mhm really"

He smirked "i look at you like i lo-

RING RING RING

i snap out of my thoughts as i see george calling me

I pick it up "Yea"

"Alexa where the fuck are you? Come on you're late.. jack is angry"

I furrow my eyebrows and said confusingly"b-but he gave off-" he cut me off

"No! He did not, now come hurry up"

"Bu-" he hung up

I sighed

I groan and changed into the skirt and formal black button down shirt

I tied my hair in a ponytail and my bangs making me look cute Oh i cut my bangs yea.Hehe i picked my purse "phone, check.. purse, check.. money, check.. keys, check"

I nodded to myself and wore my boots then i locked my door and left walking towards the cafe

I reached there soon and saw our cafe is full

What the-?

I frown and went inside looking around

Huh?

Jack came to me a really angry expression on his face "where were you?" He asked angrily

My eyed widened "i- you-" i shook my head "you messaged me saying it was off" i told him

His eyes narrowed "i never did that"

I frown and then i open my phone and readthe chat

i showed it to him "look, it is you" i said pushing my phone infront of his face

He stared at it with disbelief "i never did that" he muttered to himself

Then he pushed my hand away and said "anyhow i don't care you're still late and you will be punished, i want you in my office after restaurant close" he glared at me and left

I gulped and started my work

...

Third person's pov

(the morning of this day from george's side)

George stand infront of mirror cursing alexa and harry

"Fucking idiot what do they think of themself? I fucking love her! And she did not see it!? Fucking idiot" he yelled at the mirror

Then he opened his phone watching alexa's photo in which she is smiling sweetly He smirked "you are gonna be beaten by jack sweetheart" he hissed "oh i will love that" and he chuckled darkly

He went to jack's house early giving him some excuse jack let him in

He sat on the sofa and saw jack's phone on the table he smirked internally

Jack sat across from him

"Uh can i get water please?" George said and jack rolled his eyed then disappeared in kitchen

Looking around george quickly grabbed jack's phone then he unlocked it

Luckily it doesn't had any password

He pressed alexa's message and started writing

'The cafe will be off for today you guys don't have to come as i am not feeling really well'

He sent it quickly and removed the chat then put it on the table quickly

…

"Hey lexi what's wrong?" George asked acting like he doesn't know any-thing

She bit her lip "i don't know george. Today at morning jack messaged me saying it is off today so i slept more and you called and said it is not, when i came here i found out jack was angry and i showed him the message then jack said it was not him" she looked confused "i don't know who it could be" said deeply in thought

George smirked evily then his expression turned different "oh god i am so sorry lexi" he made a sorry expression he put his hands around her shoulder

She nodded "its okay" she looked at him and smiled shortly

...

After finishing his shift george acted like he left but he was outside the cafe

After some time alexa came her mouth bruised bleeding and her head bruised

She didn't saw george and made her way towards home

"Serves you right bitch" george muttered to himself smirking

....

Uh oh....Just imagine if harry finds out what will he doLets hope he finds out

AUTHORI am so sorry for late publishing the chapter i was really caught up with some things But i promise i will try my best and post the next chapter soon ☐

Part 7

A lexa

Who messaged me then...

I was so confused who could it be if it wasn't jackmaybe it was jack and he isn't telling me that

I went to the hospital again and she treated my wounds really well and was concerned about it but i gave her excusei walk around the street and saw it was blocked

I frown "what the-" i muttered

I took another path

The street was dark and no only dim street light was there I hugged myself and walked quietly from there

There was a whole bunch of crowd at my front there were big luxurious cars parked over there I started picking up my pace slowlyThen after walking for sometime I saw a club at my right and i stoppedI saw hot girls going inside they wore dresses that showed whole lot of their self And i think they looked sooo sexxy and beautifulI smiled at one of the girl that was looking at me she looked like my age She wore a tiny black skirt and a top that showed her cleavage

She looked beautiful

Her makeup was perfect as ever She also wore high heelsHer short hair coming down at her shoulder

She smiled and disappeared inside

I looked around at some really luxuriouscars Then i saw a really oddly familiar car parked right outside the club

I tilt my head examining it Where have i seen it?

I shrugged

What would it be like if i went inside the club

I bit my lip thinkingIt wouldn't be a crime right?

right??

I sigh and saw my clothes

I was wearing denim shorts and a simple blue button down top today My hair was in a pony tailAnd i don't even have a slightest bit of makeup

I opened my purse and saw lip glossI applied it on my lips And i opened my hair and they fall down on my shoulders and i ran a finger through itThey are nice and silkyI set my hair and wore the band on my hand

I nodded to myselfI can do this

I started walking there and i saw two big guys standing there like big.. yea, hulk type

They looked down at me

"Ma'am your id?" One of the guy that was blonde asked

I rose my eyebrows "huh?"

"your id" they repeated

I looked around

Then some girl who was blonde came at my side "she is with me" she said wrapping her arms around her chest, daring them to speak

They quickly said sorry and step out of the way

My eyes widened and i looked at her

While she smiled and took my hand then she guided us inside

The loud music was playingI smell alcohol alot of alcoholAnd i saw people dancing together some of the couples making out on couches or on the wall pressed with each other

ohkayyy

That blonde girl turned to me with a grin "hello i am isabelle" she shook my hand and i gave her a toothy grin

"Hi! I am Alexa. But lexi will go" i nodded at her"Thankyou so much for-" she cut me off by waving her hand

"Oh don't, i do it almost everyday" she chuckled and i grin

"I think im gonna catch up with my friends, you want to come?" She suggested

"Um no i think i'll drop for now but i'll join you guys some other day" i smiled

"Okay little girl" she said

"Little girl?" I giggled

"What is your age?" She asked

"Oh im 19"

She smiled and have i told you she is soo beautiful

"I am 30 darling" she said

My jaw dropped at the floor "what!" I said a little louder

She chuckled "thats the reaction of half the people"

I shook my head "no i didn't mean it li-" she cuts me

"Its okay honey i understand" she nods with a smile "im gonna give you my number we're gonna meet soon"

"Yeah sure" i gave her my phone and she feeds her number in it returning me the phone

I gave her a short hug "it was nice meeting you" i said

"Same" she said with a big smile

Then she disappeared in the crowd

I looked around and hummed at the song

It was nice but the alcohol smell was weird

I started walking further and watch all the people dressed nicely and expensive

I saw the stairs that were going up There were two bouncers there they stopped me "where are you going miss?" They asked

"Oh i-"

"Are you here to meet Mr Stewart?" They asked

I nodded without even thinking

"Yeah he said a girl wanted to meet so let her come in" one of the bouncer said to another he nodded and turned to me "you may go"

They step aside "room number 4" the said

Oh

I walked up and all doors were closed and no sound was there

Strange

I walk around and i saw room 4

I gulped and wiped my sweaty palm on my thighShould i go inside?

I held the door knob and sigh Then i twist it slowly and open it widely

The light was dim inside the room I smelt weird kind of thing and a very verryyy familiar cologne

I saw there was a bed over there And a table and a chair at the right side

A man was sitting on the chair his face in his hands A lot of white kind of powder on the table was there and i know it is drugs cocaine maybe?

"stacy" that guy said in low voice...familiar

"Why are you late.. i want you on bed now hurry the fuck up" he said "i don't have the whole fucking day, lie down you are already late"

I gulped and tiltled my head to look at him but no face was showing

"Stacy i said-" he looked up and stopped .....No fudging hell.....

Harry

His eyes widened as he took my presence

He opened his mouth to say something but nothing came outHe was wearing blue button down shirt his top 2 buttons were undone while his hair was a mess and his sleeves were rolled up He looked reallly handsome i wanna eat him-Not now alexa not now

Then when!!!

Urgh whatever

"I am not stacy" i whispered but he heard me as the room was quiet i was looking down at my shoes

I look up and he was really shocked "i think i'll leave" i said

"No, lex... its not what you think" he said his gaze now at the floor he was too embarrass to meet my eyes

"Alexa" i corrected him and his head shot up looking at me with confusion written all over his face "my name is alexa.. for you... and i don't want you to tell me anything... its not like i love you" i chuckled bitterly

I do

I didn't noticed but he was now right infront of me his tall figure towering meHis cologne filled my nose and it is like drugs to me I feel like im in heaven

"Alexa" he said and i flinched at how harshly he said it

I licked my dry lips and look up at him his jaw clenched as he glared at me"You are the guy that just go and have sex with girls and leave them" i said bitterly i was shocked i said that but i just said it and then i look at the table "and do drugs thats what your life is. Pathetic" i spat and he closed his eyes he inhale from his noseShowing he is clearly annoyed

"I want you to stay out of my fucking life..." he said in low voice his eyed find mine again "you don't know a shit and i better warn you to stay out of it do you get it?" He said gritting his teeth

I scoff "your life is a open book harry... it is your life is just as pathetic as you are" i said glaring at him

"Leave!" His voice little louder now

I didn't bulgeBut i was scared

"I said fucking leave!" He yelled and i flinched harder

Getting scared suddenly

I look up at him and saw anger in his eyes Like he wanted to kill someone so bad

He hate me doesn't he?

I smiled sadly at him "it was nice meeting yo-" he cut me off

"OUT!" He yelled louder and i flinched one more time

My eyes started to shine and i turned around leaving i rush down the stairs

My throat was feeling dry It was like i couldn't breatheMy heart started to pump louder and i couldn't hear anything just my heavy pants

I quickly went out of the club and gasped trying to breathe

My hand started to shake really badly and i looked at it with wide eye

It happens when i........panic

I gasped louder and louder

I fell on the footpath and there was no car going there no people

"No no no no no" i started to say

I felt like i was suffocating

More tears come down my eyes as i gasped louder

I saw someone appear infront of me but i couldn't see their face

They shook me "hey!!" A voice came

My eyes widened with shock

"Lexi!" Another voice came with a shake and my breathing starting to normal

I blink my tears away and saw isabelleHer face was worried

"Hey are you okay?" She asked softly and i started to cry i hugged her and cried "shh its okay.. its alright" she calmed me down But i cried harder sobbing"What happened honey" she asked and i cried more

After some time i stopped crying

"Hey lets get you home okay?" She said and i nodded

She took me to her expensive car the driver was already in it

I manage to tell her my address

Then i leaned my head on her shoulder

I closed my eyes and saw harry

I opened it immediately not wanting to see his face

The car came to a stop i turned towards her "thankyou so much" i said softly at her while she smiled

"Don't thank me" she said

Harry's words ring in my head

'Don't thank me' He said that when i thanked him for something

I shook my head

"Call me when you're feeling better okay?" She said and i nodded With a small hug i step out of the car and went inside my home

I dropped my body on the bed and criedHarder

i sob louder and my eyes started to sting

I felt helpless

I felt sad

I felt broken

Why did he.....

....

Poor alexa and harry alsoYou will get to know his side of storyThat why is he like thisThere is always a reason behind everythingI believe you should also got to know their side of story and then blame them otherwise don'tWe don't know what they're going through

Anynhow!!

Pleaseee comment down i wanna read your review i would love thatSending big hugs to you all!□□

New chapter will be up soon!

Part 8

A lexa

Its been 5 days and i haven't seen harry

I don't want to

I have been more quiet and isabelle have been by my side all the timeShe comes to my house often and i told her everything I think she is my new bestfriend

She is dating leo, i've met him, he is a nice guy and completely in love with isabelle i am really happy for her

I took a day off today because i wasn't feeling like goingI was feeling so down today

I sat on my chair and looked outside from my balconyMy hands wrap around my knees and i lay my head on it

I sigh closed my eyes and suddenly i miss dad

He was indeed the best dad He used to buy me everything i want he used to take care of me alot he used to read me bedtime stories and i used to trust him i used to tell him every thingHe was like my superhero...

A tear fall from my eye as his smiling face appears infront of my face

"Dad..." i whisper

I bit inside of my cheek "life has been really bad.. i've been feeling like total shit lately i felt like i don't have anyone.. dad you were there for me when i used to cry and when i used to get hurt you used to say don't cry honey, don't make the wound think you're weak.." i chuckle softly "i- i don't know why did you go away" i bit my lip and my eyes starter watering "i am n-nothing without you dad.." my voice breaking

I release a shaky breathe and close my eyes

I stay like that and i fall asleep..

I look around and i am in the garden

Not any garden.... My old house's garden Where dad died..

I look around and no one is there our house is still there And there is our car parked outside

I slowly take steps towards my old house then i see it is opened

I walk inside and it is decorated as same as it was when i was youngI straight go to my parents room

I open the door and i saw dad

Sitting on his armrest chair reading newspaper

My mouth agape as i watch him

He look up and smile "alexa"

I close my eyes and release a relief breathe hearing his voice

I open my eyes slowly "d-dad" i whisper

He smile widely "come sit" he gestured towards bed

I look at him for some seconds then with shaky step i reach over to bed and sit

"You've grown up" he said

I smile sadly while my eyes begin to water "y-yes"

"But you're still my little girl my lexi.." he said

I close my eyes and a tear fall "i've missed you" i said

No answer...

I open my eyes and saw dad looking down at the floor

"You haven't missed me?" I asked my voice breaking

He looked up "no...no darling i've missed you so much"

My low lip tremble

As i not believe it is real

"You know dad.... Life has been really hard since you left" i whispered looking down at my hand "why did you left?" I asked looking at him

His eyes showed guilt he shook his head "god have really great things planned for you my little girl... you have to be strong i am always there for you.. always..." he said and he start getting up

I furrow my eyebrows and wipe my tears with my palm "w-where are you going?" I ask

He just smiled sadly and start making his way backwards

I shook my head "n-no no please..." i sob and beg him "p-please don't leave me dad" i cry "i-i am all alone" i whispered

"I have no choice lexi" he said

"Please be strong for me, you are really strong don't lose hope.." he said his last words as he started to disappear

I shook my head again and again crying loud "No!! Dad!!!"

My eyes shot open and i gasp I pant as i look around

"Dad..." i said

It was a dream

I run a hand on my face and felt i cried Was the dream real? Did i really met dad?

'Please be strong for me..' his words ring in my head

He wants me to be strong to don't lose hope

"I won't..." i whisper to myself

I'll do this for you dadI will be strong for you

....

Awww Tbh i got a little emotional writing this chapter

I don't feel the pain of the people who have lost their parents

But if you are one of them

Mannn you are the strongest!! you are doing great!! And ik your parents would be so proud of you keep going and don't stop! a big hug to you guys

Im sorry for the short chapter guys but i wanted this to be a little short
Next one will be good

Loveee to you all□□Pleaseeee comment guys!! Please and also vote for the
chapter which one u think is your favourite

And comment down your fav scene till now i would love to read it!

Part 9

H ARRY's PICTURE ABOVE!

Alexa

"Alexa table number 2 " george said nicely i nodded

I gotta say george has been really really supportive since last few days i've told him all about harry and he said he is with me

What happened to him i don't know seriously but i like how he is really supportive

I walk towards table number 2 and didn't looked at who the customer is

I just hold my note pad up and ask "what would you like to have?" I ask

"You"

The notepad fell from my hand as i see harry sitting on the chair looking at me intently with those beautiful eyes i've missed his hair not properly set but look great on himHe's wearing light blue button down with black jeans

My mouth agape as i look at him he stands up

"Lex-" i cut him off by moving out of there and rushing inside the kitchen

George noticed and followed me

I pant not knowing what to do

George keep his hands on my shoulder and i flinch from his touch "Hey.. its me" george said

I did not say anything as i just keep on panting

"What happened?" He asked

"H-harry" i said my voice not even audible

He froze

"Harry is out there?" He asked

I nod

"I am gonna beat-" i cut him off

"N-no george don't go.... you are gonna lose anyways" i said

And he chuckled i also chuckled nervously

"He will go away" i told him

"You sure you don't want me to kick him out?" He asked

I shake my head and smile "thankyou george"

I hug him and he hugged me back

And suddenly he is thrown back from me

I look up and saw very furious harry

His nose flared and his veins popping out as he glare at george "How dare you hugged her" he asked gritting his teeth

George shook his head no words coming out of his mouthHe looked like he was about to piss his pants

Harry turned towards me "you like him?" He asked frowning at me

"Wha-" george cut me off

"Yes she do" he said

My mouth hang open

Harry's head snapped towards george and he step towards him while george gulped

"If i see you touching her... i will kill each one of the person you love and who is close to you infront of your eyes.." he said in low voice then he grabbed his collar "i will make them die slow and painful death infront of you and you won't be able to do anything" he harshly removed his hand and george jerked back

Harry looked at me and he didn't glared "i wanted to apologise for that da-" i cut him off as i raise my hand for him to stop talking

"I don't wanna hear anything harry, i got my answer" i said looking him straight in the eye he looked confused

"You may leave now" i look away from his eyes

He did not said anything and left

I sighed closing my eyes

"George why did you lied to him?" I ask him with concern

"I- i saved you" he said

"Wha- you-... no, you did not saved me george.. i know him before you and he won't do anything to hurt me so you shouldn't have lied" i told him

"I am sorry lexi i thought i was doing right" he apologised

I shook my head and pinched the bridge of my nose "no, its okay george really it is" i sent him a small smile and started working

...

I lay down on my bed thinking about today

Harry wanted to apologise but why?He doesn't care rightThen why

He doesn't love me nor he cares for me

I should apologise for the words i said to him but i was really angry with him

How could he ?

He is just a playboy and i fell for him

For the playboy

'when its time, when its time When its ta-ime It won't matter... it won't matter'I saw my phone ringing

Yeah i changed my ringing tone I started listening to the weeknd and his songs are amazingEspecially 'i was never there'

I saw and it was harry's number

I frown and I cut it

After some time it starts ringing again

Groaning i pick it up "What is your problem harry!" I said

"Umm hello?" Some unfamiliar voice spoke

"Hey.. who is it?" I ask pushing a strand of hair behind my ear

"Can you come at this club, mr stewart is here unconscious he is really drunk his bodyguards and everyone is gone he gave them leave so he is alone here and he is only saying one thing 'come back lex' so i took his phone and saw your contact number so i called you.. can you pick him up?" He said

"Oh god" i whisper "uh yeah sure i'll be there please text me the address"

"Right away" he said and hung up

He texted me the address and it is the one where i went last time

It was 3 in the morning It was late

I took a taxi and reached there

I asked the taxi driver to stay for awhile

I rush inside Thankfully there were no bouncers to stop me

I saw harry laying on couch his head leaned back his one arm thrown around it lazily while the other holding bottle of whiskey

"Oh my" i muttered

I walk close to him "harry" i called him

He opened his eyes and his eyes found me because of dim light i couldn't see his eyes properly "lex" he whisperedHe threw the bottle and it broke making me flinch

"Harry why are you drinking so much are you out of your mind"

"Is that really you lex?" He ask his voice deep

I sighed and walk up to him i helped him up goshh he was soo heavy

His one arm around my shoulder as i carry him outside

We step out of club "i don't wanna go home" he hiccuped

"Harry don't be ridiculous" i said

He chuckled and it send butterflies in my stomach at how nice his voice is when he chuckles "you're adorable when you're angry"

He sat down on the footpath

"For god sake! Get up we are going home" i fold my arms and glare at him

But he sat down leaning his head on the wall and at the right side there was entrance of club

He closed his eyes shaking his head

Okay so now we are acting like baby

I rub my hands on my face and groan Then i sat down beside him my knee brushing his leg

His eyes open and he look at me in the eye with his lazy eyes

Then i saw his eyes were red total red

I gasped "wha-"

I quickly cupped his cheeks "harry what happened" i whisper

He smiled sadly "i have the worst life" he said

I got closer to him biting my lip "no... don't say it like that" i said softly"What happened baby tell me" i ask

I don't know why i called him baby but i felt like it

Who hurt him i swearrrrr i will kill them without even blinking whoever hurt him

"I want you in my life lex, i want you back please" he whispered leaning in my touch

I sighed "but-"

"I promise i won't hurt you like i did but please i need you.."

I nodded without saying anywordHe needs me i am gonna help him go through whatever he is going through i kissed his forehead softly and hugged him wrapping my arm around his neck i bring him close burrying my face in his hair

"I am so sorry for what i did" harry mumbled

I shook my head kissing his top of head"Don't apologise" i said softly

I stop hugging him and cupped his cheek "lets go home okay please?" I said

He closed his eyes "okay" he muttered

With the help of taxi driver i helped him inside

He lean his head on my shoulder burrying his face in my neck sighing he kiss there softly and i blushed loving his warm lips on my neck

He stayed like that whole ride

I felt like he fall asleep but he snores softly when he sleeps and he wasn't doing that

We reached my home and i carry him inside in my apartment

He dropped his body on my bed

And he was exhausted

I sighed and remove his shoes then i walk up to him"Harry?" I said

"Hmm?" He hummed his eyes closed

"Can you get up so i could remove your shirt" i said

He chuckled "not now baby i am not in my senses now we will do it some other day" he smirked in his sleep

I frown "wha-" then i realised

I gasped "harry!"

He smirked

Then he sit up his eyes closed all the time

I slowly unbutton his shirt and removed it

Then he gets up and remove his pants leaving him in nothing but his boxers

I gulped

And i looked away

He climbed on bed laying down

I went right beside him and i covered us with comforter then i softly kissed his both eyes then i cupped one of his cheeks"Why are your eyes red" i ask softly

"Because i cried" he replied slowly

I blink and blink

I pout and laid down hugging him tightly burrying my face in his chest"Don't cry please" i mumble in his chest

Why did he cried?My poor babyyy

He chuckled and kissed top of my head "sleep"

I look up and saw his face was softened He wrap his arm around my waist pulling me more close he layed his head on top of mine

I close my eyes and snuggle close to him then i fall asleep hearing his soft snores which i love

What is that i don't love about him?

...

Why did harry cried? :(

I am so glad harry and alexa are backEven tho they are not dating but i like them together

Lets see when will they start dating each other

They haven't even had their first kissHaha, but they will kiss soon ;)

Part 10

H appy Reading.

Alexa

Its sunday today and we are now sitting on my sofa

Harry was sitting beside me his one arm wrapped around my shoulder and me curled up by his side

We were watching 'the vampire diaries'

"Don't you have any work to do today?" I ask my eyes on tv

Then i slowly look up at him and he was watching tv with focus

I shake him "hellooo chimpanzee"

His eyes snapped to me "yeah"

I pursued my lips "you didn't listen to anything i said"

He blinked "no i-" he stopped

I rolled my eyes "you don't have any work to do today?"

He clicked his tongue "no i took a day off"

I nodded

Then we started watching it again

And i realised

Why am i so curled up and cuddly with him?

He does not love me

And he had sex with some girl that day

Instantly anger burns inside me and i back off from him

And sat up folding my arms i glared at him

He turned his head slowly towards me and smiled sheepishly "what happened?" He ask innocently like he doesn't know anything

Oh reallyyyyy???

I paused the series and continue to glare him

"Sweetheart you have to talk to me if i did anything wrong... which i don't know what i did" he said last part slowly slightly confused

"You.slept.with.the.girl" i narrowed my eyes at him

He furrow his eyebrows "wha-" i cut him off

"You did! Ha! I knew it i knew it!" I yelled

And his eyes widened

"You don't know what am i planning in my mind to do to you right now"

He opened his mouth but i stopped him

"No... no don't you dare try to tell me you didn't have sex with her! Oh cause i know!!" I nodded "yeah i know that you did!" I yelled "i want to cut your irritating chimpanzee head off right now and feed it to.. to..." i think a little "yes! To a gorilla" i grin evilly

"I did not have sex with her" he said in boring tone

"You did, and then you come back to me, and may i ask why?"

He took his cigarette pack out and then took on cigarette out and lit it "cause i missed you" he said and smoke

I gasped "You are smoking in my Apartment!! In my apartment!!??"

He frown

"Get.out" i said

"You need to calm-" i cut him off

"No either you throw that away or you get out of my apartment" i said pointing him with my finger

He groan "fine" he gave the pack to me and his cigarette also "happy?" He raised his hands in surrender

I rolled my eyes and threw the packet away

I sat down on sofa again and little far from him

"Now tell me, how many girls have you had sex with?" I ask with curiosity

He frowns "i don't know"

I glare at him "Speak"

He pursue his lips and think "i mean 20? Or 25? I don't know"

My eyes widened and they almost pop out of socket "are you serious?"

"I am not sure maybe more than this" he shrugged

He is acting so casual like it is nothing

Oh are you kidding me man

"Out of my house" i said

"Listen" i tried to speak but he didn't let me "let me speak for fuck sake"

I sigh "okay"

"So yes i did have sex with them but no i have got not any single feelings for one of them i have sex with them when i am stressed or when i am really done with everyone then i call them or i go to the club and have sex with them and i never see their faces again having sex well that releases my tension and stress" he explained

I made a disgusting face "but that is really weird harry.. i... i mean you could talk to someone to release you from whatever stress you are having which god knows what it is but this is not any solution"

He didn't answer

I sighed "and about drugs and drinks? Is that good?"

"Yeah i don't think about anything... what i meant to say is i don't stress if i take drugs or drink... soo..... there you have it" he release a breathe running a hand in his hair

I shook my head and got a little closer to him i touch his shoulder and he looked at me in the eye without any emotion

"Look harry... " i run my fingers on my forehead and sighed "doing all these things aren't gonna ease your problems they are just gonna make it more worse, having sex taking drugs, drinking... that is not..... good and it is uh.. really bad for your health except sex it is okay i mean it does not harm Your health but you could've saved it for someone who is worth it" i look back and forth between his two eyes trying to explain him "and talking about stress then you can release it any other way by running... it reduces your stress or by gymming extra there are many other solutions then these, the one that you chose are the worst ones"

He nodded slowly "yeah.. i think you're right" he mumbled i smiled slightly "but i am addicted to it lex... there's nothing i can do"

I bit my lip

This isn't right alexa don't be stupidOne voice spoke in my mind

No i mean i can do this for harry? Right?Another voice spoke in my mind

Shut up alexa you have never thought about it how are you gonna?

I will do this for harry

No-

"I can be one of your solution" i said biting my lip and looking down at my hand

Not meeting his eyes

He put his finger under my chin and made me look at him "what are you saying?" He asked in slow voice

"I... i mean i can... uh.." i clear my throat "you can have s-sex with me" i said biting my lip

He looked at me for some second and then he chuckled "what" Not believing what i said

"That will solve one of your problem right? And you don't have to find any other girl sooo... there's that"

He cupped my cheeks "thankyou so much for saying that lex... thankyouu really much but i can't take advantage of you... you are.. different from all the girls and i... i can't use you" he shook his heads and then he kissed my forehead and he pressed his forehead with mine and sighed he closed his eyes not saying anything

"harry" i whispered

He hummed

"I love you" i said softly

He froze and then he opened his eyes slowly

He backed off and watched me with his shocking expression "you love me?" He asked

I nodded

He frowns "no, you.. you can't love me lex i.... I don't deserve love"

"No.." I moved forward and tried to touch his cheek but he backed off

I looked at him with my mouth opened a little

I backed off and looked down at my hands "you do deserve love" i whispered

He run his hands on his hair and groan "you shouldn't have loved me lex! I am a MOTHERFUCKER!" He yelled and i flinch "DON'T YOU

KNOW THAT I AM A FUCKING BAD PERSON!? DON'T YOU SEE?" He yelled louder and i whimper a little scared of him

"I FUCKING HURT PEOPLE! I FUCKING BREAK THEM INTO PIECES!" he stood up and i watched him with fear

"You know the people i love? I fucking break them" he said in low voice

"WHY DID YOU LOVED ME!?" He yelled again louder

"N-no i- i don't l-love you" i said softly trying to calm him down

He chuckled bitterly "DON'T FUCKING LIE TO ME!"

I flinch and tears start to form in my eyes

He rubbed his hands on his face "FUCK!"

A sob escape my mouth and i quickly put a hand on my mouth

Harry looked at me and he started coming close i flinch and back

"Lex.. are you crying?" He ask softly

He touched my cheeks but i flinch louderHe quickly removed his hands

"D-don't hurt me please..." i shut my eyes tightly

I opened my eyes and saw harry's face showing guilt and his eyes telling he is veryy sorry

"I- i didn't mean to-" i cut him off

"You scared me.." i bring my knees close to my chest "h-harry p-please don't.." my voice barely audible

"No..no i won't hurt you baby.. i won't" he whispered his face showing guilt "You don't deserve me" he cupped my cheek and i didn't flinch he caressed it "you deserve someone you won't hurt you... i am a motherfucker lex and i know no matter how hard i try i will hurt you..." he removed his hands

"But i love you harry... d-do you?" I ask

He didn't answered and start getting up

"Where are you going?" I ask

"I am leaving and i won't come back" he looked up at me "i am sure you'll find a great guy... bye lex" he said and left

I watch the door as it shut with my mouth agape and my eyes started watering the tears start running down and i just stare at the door without saying anything

I was helpless

again

.....

Okayyy that was........

Idk it was mixed emotion

What do y'all think does harry love lexi? If he does then he shouldn't have left her righttt?

sigh well lets see what is gonna happen now

Love you alll □

Part 11

<hr>

H^{arry}

I call one of the whores today at my home

She'd be coming by now

Door bell rang and one of the maid open it

I was in my room

Since 2 days i've been in my room all the fucking timeLex told me that she loves meAnd i was out of words I was angry that how could a certain person love me? me?

My room door opened and logan came inside

I rolled my eyes "why are you here?"

He came and sat on the bed "bro what the fuck is wrong with you? You aren't coming to work you aren't attending IMPORTANT business meetings? What the fuck happened?" He asked with whole serious face

I know he wasn't joking And i was acting like that

I had no mood to do fucking business

My jaw clenched as i shut my eyes "you don't know what i am going through" i told him

"Then fucking tell me! Why do you call me your bestfriend when you ain't gonna tell me shit" he said a little louder

I sighed and took a glass of cold water then drank it relaxing my mind

"Okay i am gonna tell you" i told himHe nodded eagerly waiting for me to explain

A knock interrupted me "come in" i said

And a girl walked in she was wearing a whole big coat covering her body

Okay so she's the one i called

"Should we start?" She asked in seductive voice

She looked at logan and bit her lip "oh threesome?"

Logan burst out with laughter while i shook my head at him

I clear my throat "i don't wanna do anything" i said

She gasped "why did you called me then!"

I run my finger through my hair "first of all voice down bitch and second of all i changed my mind"

"My mone-" before she could finish

I gave her the money practically throwing it on her

She took it and rolled her eyes

"Be careful with that attitude you are gonna be dead if you threw that sass on the wrong guy..you should thank me for not ripping your throat out... now fuck off"

She quickly rushed and left

Logan turned towards me "oh so you started calling whores!?" His mouth drop "are you fucking kidding me? Yeah we use to fuck girls but not daily!"

I rolled my eyes "listen to me?"

"Go on i am all ears"

"So starting off with my dad, you know i don't have any good relations with him since i was 10 because he married someone else just because my mom died" i scoffed "well you know that so my stepmother Claire.. she doesn't like me not even a bit and i don't give two fucks about it but she started to lie to my dad that i bring girls at home and i take drugs and i drink... dad confronted me with that and i said what was truth i said no.. i knew it was claire who did all this so i called her a 'whore' which dad didn't liked so he slapped me and he is asking for the half of the property to name it on claire... i would do it over my dead body" i said clenching my jaw "he doesn't know that i've caught her many times with many guys and she tried to fucking seduce me so i don't tell dad... and then i started doing all those things that she said i took drugs i fuck girls in this house and i fuck them so hard that she hear their voices and i drink.. dad knows about it now and he haven't spoken to me about the property yet" i said pinching the bridge of my nose

"Man that is fucked up... but why do you proved claire right? Why didn't you told dad that she is lying?" He asked

"I tried okay? I tried to tell him but" i scoffed "he didn't give a shit about what i say"

He shook his head "we need to think about something now you can't keep doing these shit"

I didn't answer

"And what about that girl.. uh..... yeah! Alexa"

I froze

"She told me that she loved me" i blurted

"WHAT?"

"Yeah... and i.." i clench my jaw inhaling

"Me being a fucking coward i backed off i left her"

"What the fuck bro? You seriously did that?"

"I know i fucked up but i dont want to hurt her okay? I don't-" i stopped and gulped "you know that i hurt the ones i love right?" I ask

"No bro you don't do it intentionally" he said trying to support me

"NO! I FUCKING DO IT INTENTIONALLY" i yelled

My body burns with anger

"Okay... calm down" he said nodding

After some time i spoke"You remember i told you about my birth mom" looking at my wrist

It has a tattoo of her name liana

"Yes i remember" he said quietly

Flashback

Mom comes and kissed me on forehead "you promise to behave when we go there?" She asks

I nod "yes mama"

She grins "that is my boy"

"But mama i don't want to go. They doesn't like me" i said looking down

"No harry.. they like you they do... if you don't come with me i am gonna be hurt" She said

"Mama please" i begged

I didn't wanted to go at 'the Walton's' house they planned a dinner today at their houseTheir kids hate me they always bully me and say bad things about me

"Harry-" i cut her off

"Mama" i said with pleasing voice

She sighed "okay.. but i am hurt you hurt me by not coming with me" she said pouting a little

"I am gonna make it up to you" i said

"Oh are you?" She asked

I nodded "yes"

She likes cake alot so i am gonna make a cake with the help of our chef

"Okay then when i'll be back then i'll decide if i am still hurt or not"

I grinned and she kissed my forehead then she left

She sat in car and i waved at herDad wasn't home today so driver took her

I went back to my room and played with my car

...

After some time...

"HARRY!" Dad's called me from downstairs

"HARRY WHERE ARE YOU!?" He yelled

He sounded angry

I quickly rushed downstairs and saw dad He was looking messy his tie not tied right

His suit jacked off his hair a mess

He glared at me "WHY DID YOU LET HER GO ALONE?" He yelled and i flinch

"D-dad what are you s-saying" i said quietly

Not understanding what he was saying

"YOU KILLED HER! YOU DID! YOU BASTARD!" He slapped me hard across the face and i start crying "OH NOW YOU ARE CRYING? AFTER TAKING HER AWAY FROM ME!?"

He shook me hard "TELL ME!?"

I sobbed "i-i don't know d-dad"

he opened the tv "LOOK!" he yelled and i looked at the tv

A news was playing

"There was a bomb blast at the **** bridge (Guys i didn't knew what to write the bridge's name haha so it is censored sorryy)A car was blasted and the report tells that there was a driver and a woman.. yes a woman.. named Liana Stewart Unfortunately she died and the driver named David Teir also died Their bodies are now being collected We have contacted their families and our condolences to the families..."

Dad switched the tv off

I was out of words as i fell down on floor i started crying "mama"

"YOU KILLED HER BECAUSE OF YOU! SHE DIED! YOU DIDN'T GO WITH HER YOU LET HER GO ALONE YOU DIDN'T EVEN STOPPED HER!! WHY!!!" He yelled and slapped me again kicking me on the stomach i groan with pain and cried

Mom's word rang in my head 'I am hurt.... You hurt me by not coming with me'

Flashback ended

I gasped as i shook away thoughts

"Dude but she didn't meant that you know she was joking" he consoled me

I smile humourlessly "i wish i stopped her that day or i wish i could've gone with her" i told him "first i hurt my mom then my dad the two people i loved the most... "

Logan came up to me and hugged me i pat his back

Then we backed off

"Now we gotta think what to do with that bitch claire.. and you kindly motherfucker stop doing these things" he said

I chuckled "alright"

"Andd.. make it up to alexa" he said

"No i can't do that she surely hates me now" i shook my head

"No she do not hate you.. the main point is do you love her?" He asked

I rubbed the back of my neck smiling a little

"You are whipped!!" He chuckled patting my back

I smile "i do love her... i love her so fucking much... her smile her laugh her eyes everything about her i fucking love her... just afraid to tell her"

"You are gonna do it or else i'll do it" he said

I glare him "you'll be 6 feet under if you tried to get close to her"

"Yeah! That's my boy" he pat my shoulder "now come on action time babyyy"

Okayy

I am gonna do it..

....

Backstory of harry

I felt bad for harry

He deserve so much better

Will alexa forgive harry??

Lets see

Until next chapter guyssssss it will be up soon tho

Love y'all☐

Part 12

A lexa

Owww

Jack slapped me again and again on my right cheek

Becauseeee

Well i took 2 days off i was not feeling well i had a fever and jack mr small dick isn't believing me Why would i lie?

And another slap

Smackk

"You are not gonna take another leave do you get me??" He ask

I was not looking in his eye i nodded hurriedly

"If you did then you don't want to know what i'll do to you" he said slowly

I nodded again

He grabbed my hair and i pressed my lips together not to screamHe grabbed it harshly cause my scalp burn now

"YOU MOTHERFUCKER!" I heard familiar voice coming from behind

Within a second jack was thrown back from me

I release a breathe then and i opened my eyes to see

Harry punching the life out of jack

"Harry!" I rush towards him "leave him harry you're gonna kill him" i said bringing him back

Harry finally backed off glaring him burning holes in his head his jaw clenched and his nose flared "How the fuck did you touched her" he gritted his teeth

He grabbed jack's throat choking him

I put a hand on his forearm trying to remove it "please don't do it harry!"

He harshly removed it and jack fell down

His mouth and nose were bleeding he coughed and more blood came out

He turned towards me "he used to fucking beat you and you never told me" he asked not yelling but in serious voice

I shook my head "h-harry i....i couldn't tell you"

He came towards me and cupped my cheeks i made contact with his beautiful eyes "you could've told me lex i don't even know since when he is beating you like this" he backed off and pulled his hair in frustration

"But look i am fine" i gave him weak smile

He looked at me and his eyes clearly showed he does not believe me

He grabbed my arm and i followed him till outside He opened his car door for me

"I am not coming with you" i said

He frowns "why?"

"Well because you said we can't happen and you left me.. that is why" i folded my arms

He sighed "i want to talk about some stuff with you lex please.. just sit in the car"

"Where are we going?"

"My home"

I shook my head "no.. never happening"

He groans "just sit inside.. for heaven's sake"

"You are gonna buy me donut then" i said biting my lip

His eyes flick down to my lips he gulped "yeah" he looked up at my eyes

I sat inside and his car is filled with his rich cologne

He sat in driver's seat and closed the door

He looked at me for a second then he stretch his arm in the backseat and there was his suit jacket

He cover me with his suitjacket i smiled at him

He started driving

"So do you live with your parents?" I ask him

He grip the steering wheel tightly his knuckles turning white

"I-its okay if you don't want to answe-"

"Yes. But they are out of city"

I nodded "okay"

"Where does your parents live?" He asked

I start fiddling with my fingers

His hands cover mine and he interwined our fingers i smiled looking at our hands

"I live alone... my father died and my mother.." i sighed "i don't wanna talk about it... is it fine" i looked up at him

"Yeah.. sure" he said softly

Harry bought me donuts and he asked for some parcel Goshhhh i love him

After that we reached the destination And Oh My God

He have a fudging mansion!! There were many guards outside his mansion when they saw harry they saluted him and they opened the door

There is a big statue of lion at the entrance when you enter inside there is a big roundabout a lady holding a tea kettle and water is falling from it Then there is a big ass garden Its dark so i can't see the beauty of it then there is a garage Harry drive the car slowly and took it inside his garage

There are so many luxurious car parked And all black

He parked his car and then we get out of his car

My mouth fall open as i look over all his cars "Wow" i whisper

I looked at harry he had a small smile on his face

How can someone be so cuteeee

He grabbed my hand and started leading me inside of his mansion

We walked inside and it was all soo clean and beautiful There was a huge chandelier hanging in the middle of the hall The floor was white and clean There were two stairs going up they were really big and looked great

I walked inside and at my right i saw there was lounge area It had expensive sofas over there following with a huge tv hanging on the wall There was a big window throw which you can see outside

At my left i saw there was a big dining table and so elegant There was a collidor inside which i couldn't see but i started walking there and harry followed me without saying anything

The collidor was big ass

From collidor starting at my right i saw there was the kitchen a really nicely modern designed kitchen

Then after leaving kitchen there were many rooms

I looked at harry "what are these rooms?" I asked him

He shoved his hands in his pockets "some of it are of our servants while when you walk further in there is guest rooms"

I nodded "oh"

"Should we go upstairs now?" He asked

I nodded happily

He took us to the middle of the hall and except going from the stairs

There was a fudging elevator...yeah... elevator inside his mansion

"Harry we can go from the stairs" i said to him

"My room is on third floor"

I frown "third?"

"Yes"

We get inside elevator and he pressed 3rd floor There were 4 floor

"What is on the 4th floor?" I asked him

"Swimming pool and roof" he said

I nodded biting my lip

Wow

The elevator dings and it opened showing 3rd floor

I gasp looking around it was sooooo big and amazing

I followed him to the right and he stopped infront of some room i bumped into his back he pushed the passwords and then some robot spoke 'Password Correct'

His door opened and i gasp again

His room was so large It had black theme

There was a king sized bed laying following with gorgeous nightstands there was a table at the right following with the armchair and then there was a window it showed outside viewI walk there and saw the view was amazing

"You like the view?" Harry asked

"Yeah" i breathed

"Make yourself comfortable i'll be back" he said and disappeared in the washroom

I slowly sat on his bed and woahh it was all jumpy kind of bed

I jumped on it grinning

then i jumped and jumped

And harry came out of bathroom he looked at me and i stopHe smirked He was changed in his sweatpants and grey shirt

He came to sit on the bed his back was leaned back on the headboard

He pat his side "come"

I crawled there and sat beside him looking at him

"You wanted to talk" i said

He nodded "yeah"

What will he say?

....

So sorry for the cliffhanger!! But i promise next chapter will be up soon!

Love y'all

Part 13

A lexa

we were looking at each other since past 5 minutes and i am so lost in his beautiful eyes that i don't care about the worldI don't care about the birds chirping or the wolf howling i don't care about even the damnnn donutsCan you believe that?I meanWow

I clear my throat "harry i thought you wanted to talk about some stuff" i said

He nodded running his hand on the back of his neck "yeah.."

I leaned my side on the headboard and my body was fully turned towards him

He opened his mouth and started explaining me about all the stuff about his dad and his step momI was really shocked when he tell me about his birth mom And i felt really immensely bad for what he have gone through

I nodded all the way as he explains me everything perfectly

"....soo this is what i wanted to talk about" he start tracing his finger on his another palm

"And why did you.... leave me?" I ask biting my lip

He didn't look up nor he say anything he just release soft breaths

I scoot closer "harry i need to know okay... i.. i was hurt"

His eyes snap up to me and his eyes was wide with horror as his mouth was opened a little he looked at me like he didn't believe what i said

"I.... I did what i was afraid of" he whispered his voice barely audible

"What?" I look at his face studying him

He was like a puzzle I was trying so hard to solve

"I....hurt you" he flinched at his own words

"You didn't" i put a hand on his arm "hey... you didn't hurt me okay?" I said softlyI kissed his forehead

"But you said-" i cut him off

"Forget what i said okay? I speak nonsense" shaking my head i told him

A ghost of smile touching his lips

"Now tell me please?"

He sighed running his hands on his hair he told me all about the thing 'hurt'

What i mean to say is he thinks he hurts everyone he loves

I frown at him when he finishes

"What...no you don't stop blaming yourself for heaven's sake harry" i said frowning at him

He shrug "i can't help it"

"You won't hurt me im sure now shutup with that stupid theory"

He chuckles his hair falls on his forehead and his dimples showing

Wh-Di-No-

HE HAVE FREAKING DIMPLES

he's so cute I am screaming internally

He looks at me and then he cups my cheek caressing it his eyes flick down to my lip "you know.. whenever i see you.. i always want to kiss you" he said he leaned closer still looking at my lips "i want to kiss the life out of your lips lex" his eyes looked up at me and he was asking for my permission

I gulped

I bit my lip and nod

Then Mr Harry Chimpanzee was sold

he pressed his soft lips to mine i felt fudging fireworks in my stomach

What the heck

He start moving his lips slowly around my lips and i did the same following his movement i curl my hand in his hair bringing him close to me.. impossibly close

His hands find my waist and he pulls me to him tighterHe sneak his tongue inside my mouth and i feel his tongue and godddd he taste like heaven

We kissed enjoying each other for some timeBut we need to breathe or else we'll die.. yea die die

We back off from kiss our forehead pressed we both pant

"I loved that" he mumbled

I smiled

"I also liked it" i lick my lips tasting him

"Gosh i love your lips" he leans and kiss me softly then taking my bottom lip in his teeth softly tugging it

"Lex... i fucking love you" he whispered

I froze and looked at him in the eye trying to find any joke but no humour in his eyes

"I love you so much that sometimes it aches me to love someone this much... i can't let you go the fool i am... because you're an angel, an angel send to me and i will never leave this angel ever.... and ik its really late to ask but Alexa Will you be my girlfriend?" He asks

And i felt another huge fireworks in my stomach

I bit my lip then i grinned widely at him and cupped his cheek i kissed him "i love you too Harry i love you really much...and yes i'll be your girlfriend" i squeal in excitement

As he looke at me with a really gorgeously sexy grin on his face

We're officially dating. Yay!!

I wrap my arm around his neck and bring him close to me hugging him loving the warmth and closenessHis head was on my neck taking soft breaths i felt it and butterflies launched in my stomach..again

I backed off from hug "oh i need shirt i need to change" i said looking down at my clothes he nods

"Yeah sure" he said and stood up going in his walk in closet

He came back with black shirt he gave it to me i smiled at him

He came back sitting on bed his head leaned back on headboard looking at me

I stood up and start unbuttoning my shirtHarry looks at me and raises his eyebrows "darling what are you doing?"

I removed my shirt and start uncliping my bra "changing" i said carefully unclipping it

"OH DEAR GOD" he screams as his eyes went wild he quickly puts his hand on his eyes

I furrow my eyebrows

Drama princess queen

"Infront of me??" He asks his hands still covering his eyes as his brows furrow

I stare at him with 'seriously?' look but he couldn't see me as his dumbass covered his hands with his eyesI wear this shirt without bra but it was black so you couldn't see clearly"I've changed" i said and he removed his hands slowly opening his eyed

"No seriously what is wrong with you" he asks his nose scrunched up

I will eat you if you became more cuter than you already areStop being that cute!!

"We are dating aren't we?" I ask folding my arms looking at him raising my eyebrows

He nodded his nose still scrunched up

Oh shutup cute ass person

"So i can change infront of you and you've already seen many girl's boo bs..... and i don't have anything other attached there" i said, making sure i peek inside and nod to myself

"No i mean.. we haven't had sex and all and if i saw you naked" he gulped"Well then" he fake coughs "you know what will happen"

I smirk "oh yeah? Tell me what will happen?"

He smirked back looking sexy He licked his lips "should i show you?" He asks

I sat on bed and shook my head grinning

"Noo i will show you" he quickly pull me down and i squeal with surprise he hovers my body and looked at me evilly i looked up at him

Then he started tickling me i giggle "stop!" I started laughing

He looked at me grinning while tickling me

"Harry p-please" i laugh "i can't breathe!!" He stops and kissed my forehead

I pant and he lays down beside me "how was it babygirl?" He asked winking

I giggle "amazing" i kissed his lips softly

"Told ya" he snap his finger at me smirking

I chuckled

Then he turned his tv on and i cuddle with him

Laying my head on his chest my leg on his leg and his arm around my waist Comforter draped on us I snuggle closer to him and he kiss the top of my head stop ittt or i'll explode with how much fireworks are happening in my stomach

I love him so much

I would choose him over anyone again and again

...

SooooooHow was the chapter my loves????

I tried my best to not disappoint you guys !

Love y'all□Next chapter will be up soon! ;)

Part 14

A lexa

I wake up rubbing the back of my hand on my right eye

"Good morning love" i saw harry smiling at me standing infront of the bed "i brought you breakfast" he nods at my side i look there and a cart was there the breakfast was on it i look back at him and he was all dressed up He's wearing black suit his hair properly combed but still falling on his forehead making him look extraa cute his tie is looking like he had a hard time tying it

I chuckle as i open my eyes lazily smiling at him

He looks at himself and looks back at me "whats wrong"

I crawl towards him and he froze looking at me His throat working as his eyes alarmed watching my every move His eyes move down to my body and he exhale harshly

I am a tease

I sat on my knees looking up at him while he looked down at me

"Come here" i whisper

He raises his eyebrow "what are you doing?" He ask in low voice

"Don't worry i won't bite"

He broke eye contact brushing his hair with his finger muttering something under his breathe but i heard it "i wish u do"

I giggle at him

"Lean down please" i said

"Baby if you want a kiss just ask me why doing all this-"

I groan "harry please" i say

He leans down and i look in his eyes grey eyes, so beautiful eyes i start removing his tie and his eyes widened he back off "you are horny in the morning?" He asks frowning

I bit back a smile "what" i ask innocently

He sighed "i have work to do darling and i can't do it..... now.... when i come back" he smirks "well we'll-" i cut him off by laughing hard My head thrown back as i laugh looking at him

He looks confused

Really confused

"D-did you really thought i wanted to have sex?" I laugh again

He blinks at me while frowning deeply

I giggle "i was teasing you, your tie wasn't tied nicely so i thought i should give you a little hand"

He bit his lips trying his hardest not to smile clearing his throat he held a serious face "well now i need your little hand but not on my tie..." he looks down and i follow his gaze looking at his.......................pants?

My eyes widened with realisation "w-what" my voice barely audible

He bring his head up smirking at me He step forward while i couldn't speaktoo stunned to speak..

He leans down and his nose touching mine i gulped

He licks his lips "what do you think darling?"

"huh?" I stare at him in shock

his eyes were laughing Thenhe started laughing

How can someone have such a cute angelic laugh ? What the-

He throw his head back as he laughs

He stopped laughing "gotcha" he winks

I shook my head "you-" he cuts me off

"what? Handsome? Sexy? Immensely gorgeous?" He asks smiling at me

"Yeah all that but you idiot"

He grins

"Okay now i gotta head to work, i'll be back soon" he leans in and kisses me softly then he kisses my forehead cland turns to leave

"Wait what am i gonna do?" I asked

He stops and turn around "hmm, you can explore the house, whatever you want"

I nod "do you have a gym?"

He tilt his head looking at me carefully "ofcourse sweetheart it is in the basement"

"okay" i smile "you may go now"

He raise his eyebrows, amusement dancing in his eyes then his eyes calm "yes ma'am"

I giggle and he winks at me then left...

I sat up stretching then i looked at my left the huge window

I slowly go there and saw the viewIts so beautiful

I've been here for what feels like an eternity

I turn and made my way towards the washroom

I should take a shower

I put my hand on the right side of neck than crack it

I strip off clothes and went inside showering

I saw body wash there And it is what harry uses

I grin to myself and use it

Now im gonna smell like him

I shower off then i wrap a towel around myself And i walk out of the bathroom There was a collidor leading to what looks like room?

I go there as lights open by itself and i gaspWoahhhIt is a walk in closet and it is huge but a little small from his room

I open his closet and saw his expensive suits there following with his watches his belts his shoes and his tiesI open another closet and there was his casual clothes I grab his blue t shirt and his sweatpants

I giggle to myself as i saw his hoodie

Not now its not winter yetI'll come back for you buddy

I wore his clothes and it smell like him I smell like him well not fully as he also uses his expensive colognes/perfumes I don't know where they are, sadly

My hair fall freely down and i walk back in the room eating the breakfast

After breakfast i made my way to the elevator then i pressed basement floor (ground floor)

I open my phone and took selfie pouting then i took one winking at the camera while grinning i took more selfies

Ding

Okay here we are

The elevator opened and my mouth fall open

Oh My God

This gym have every machine i want No one was here

This gym was hugeee

I tie my hair up in a bun and i start exercising doing my cardio, yoga and then running on treadmillLifting some weights

I look at my phone and i've been here since 2 hours

I saw towels hanging i took one and wiped all my sweat

Then a thought came to me

I just showered You just showered Alexa

I groan

Then i push the elevator's button and it was on 3rd floor

I tap my foot as it comes down

Then i enter inside and went to where harry's room is

I showered again and changed in his other sweatpants and white shirt

I put the clothes i wore in what looks like laundry basket

I sat back down on the bed and called harry

"Hello" his sexy voice

"Hii how are you?" I ask

I hear him chuckle "baby you saw me 2 hours ago how was i then?"

"Handsome" i blurt out

He chuckles again "i am great what are you upto?"

I told him i showered 2 times and he laughed a little

"So when are you gonna be back?" I ask

"I'll be back in 1 hour"

I grin then i bite my lip "okay come fast"

"Okayy bye sweetheart" his voice soft

My heart

"Bye" i hung up

I laid on the back sighing closing my eyes

Then my eyes shot open

I did not went to work and george also didn't called me

Shit shit shit shit shit shit shit

All of this shitttttttAll of itExcept harryAll of this is fudging shitt Ahhhhh

....

Part 15

H arry

"We're here sir" my driver robert said i nodded

"Thankyou robert" he smiled brightly

I get off the car and he took the car to garage I ring a bell and a maid came to open the door she greeted me and i nodded

My baby must be upstairs

I got in elevator and it took me to my floor

The elevator opened and i stepped out, the only voice that i heard was of my shoes

i slowly twisted the door knob after pushing the passwords, speaking of passwords i told lex the password of my room so she don't face any trouble

the first thing my eye caught was the room's light was dim i stepped inside slowly closing the door slowly

i saw small figure laying on the bed all curled up

What happened my baby

I slowly walk there and sat down beside alexaHer hair was falling on her face i couldn't see her face i couldn't see her gorgeous blue eyes I dragged her hair at the back of her ear and caressed her cheek She was frowning, yeah

"Darling" i said in slow voice

she backed off

I froze blinking trying to figure out thatWhat the hell just happened

She sat up pushing her hair away

Damnn

"Open the lights" she said without looking at me

I look at my right my left

Oh she's talking to me, what a good day

I stood up and took a remote turning the lights on I turn back looking at her

Wait can you explain me How can one person be so pretty?

I walk up to her and sat down again

She folded her arms still frowning but this time looking at her lap

I release a breathe and touch her arm which she pushed away

"What's wrong?" I ask literally confused

I didn't do anything wrong did i?

You didn't buy her flowers dickheadOne thought came to me

Oh shit

"Is it about flowers? I am sorry sweetheart i literally forgot, i should go back and bring-" she cut me off

"Huh?" She tilted her head "flowers?"

I nodded "you're angry because of that right?"

"What? No!"

She sighed "im not angry because of the damn flowers, you DID not told me i had work to do!....and... Oh god! It slipped of my mind and you did not told me!" She said totally upset

"Well it-" she cuts me off AGAIN

"You didn't told me nor i remembered it.. shittt. Jack is gonna kill me" she say biting her thumb

"If he touches you he will be fucking dead" my voice dangerously low as i stare at the wall glaring at it like it is jack

"What will i do??" She asked in her scary tone

"First of all calm down, and come here" i opened my arms and she gladly took the invitation and wrapped her arms around my neck as she straddled me sitting on my lap

i ran my fingers on her smooth silky hair "don't worry, i'll talk to him" i mumble

She backed off still sitting on my lap "nooo you'll beat him" her eyes widened "please don't"

I clenched my jaw and made contact with her eyes "alexa, if he touches you..... i would gladly put a bullet through his skull and choke him to death... if anyone touches you"

She looked down nodding slowly

I put my finger on her chin bringing her head up wanting to meet her gorgeous blue eyes"I didn't kissed you and im dying" i pressed my lips to her softly moving it around her lips as she taste like cherrysweet cherry

She bring her arm up my shoulder as she tilt her head back i stop kissing her and move my mouth down her sweet neck softly sucking there she moaned a little

Fuck

I stop kissing her and looked at her she looked confused

"Some other day" i whisper as i kiss her lips again but for a little

-Alexa

We are now laying on his bed But not asleep

He then sits up and i also do "What happened?" I ask

"Where is your phone?" He asked then he saw it was beside me and he grab it

"Harry give me my phone back" i say trying to snatch my phone

Well it was too late

He opened my phone and then went into Gallery

I did not argue or anything i just watch him looking at my phone

He raises an eyebrow and smiles when he saw my pictureIn this picture i am laying on bed and i've made a sad pouting face

The backstory is i had to work on sunday also so i took a picture of me sad

He watched the pictures i took today

"You're so cute" he said his eyes focused on my phone on meI blushed

He send himself my pictures

Then he give me my phone back i raise my eyebrow at him as he opened his phone and updated his wallpaper with my picture the one which in which im winking

"Harry this is the worst picture" i lied

It was the bestttt

But i wanted his wallpaper to be his and mine's picture

"No fuck off" he said as he laid down again

I shook my head as i laid with him

"Harry drop me home tomorrow" i mumble as i look up at ceiling

"Stay" he say

"I have work to do and i...i can't always spend the night at your house daily"

He sighed "i'll see about it"

I frown "bu-"

He kisses my lips softly "sleep baby"

I sighed and turned around so i could be the little spoon

I smiled as i went to sleep

Sleeping with harry's arm around me is the best sleep i get

.....

Next chapter will be updated soon!Keep voting please i love you all

Part 16

A lexa

Harry dropped me home after me convincing him with a kiss

Wellll

He asked for it

i choose to meet grandma today Yeah the grandma i met at apartment I met her a week ago

I bought a bouquet of roses for her

I smiled at the bouquet thinking of how happy she'll get

I arrived at the apartment

And i get inside the elevator The memory hit me

Me and harry met here for the first time

I grinned at the thought

I pressed 22 floor

I got off the elevator going to grandma's home

I rang the bell and grandma appeared

She grinned as she saw me and embrace me in a warm hug

"Sweetheart its so good to see you" she said

I smiled "i missed you"

"I also missed you honey come in" she stepped aside so i could come in

I get inside her apartment sitting in her lounge area

"What do you need for drink?" She asked

"No no i don't need any drink" i chuckle "i just came to meet you"

"No darling im still gonna bring you a drink" she smiled

"But grandma-" she didn't listen to me and went inside her kitchen

After a minute she brought orange juice with her

"Thankyou so much" i say taking the glass

"Oh silly girl don't thank me drink up now" she waved her hand off

I chuckled and drink the juice

"How have you been?" She asked

"Oh life has been pretty weird and good at the same time... i..am well in love with a guy" i blushed as i tell her this

"Oh my! Really?" She seemed excited

"Yes, and he is really caring and i love him so much i can't even explain"

"What are your plans for wedding then?" She asked

"Uh wedding? Well we haven't talked about it and i don't think harry will like the wedding too soon" i said

"Harry?" She asked

I nodded "yeah his name is harry, harry stewart"

She stood up with shock "harry?? Oh god! He is my grandson!" she exclaimed

My eyes widen "What!"

"Yes! He is my grandson and he comes to meet me here" she say

I grinned and hugged her "thats so cool!" I chuckled not believing it

"That is such a great coincidence" she said

I nodded agreeing with her

"I am gonna come often then to meet you and you're gonna actually be my grandma" i say

"That is great having you as harry's wife will be really great to me! And i am really happy for you two" she kissed my head and i smiled

After talking about alot of things with grandma i decided to leave as it was a little late now

I went to my house and decided to call harry

"Harry" i say

"Look who decided to call"

I frown

Is he on man's period

"Well i went to meet someone" i bit my lip

"Meet who?"

I clear my throat "this is gonna sound weird but i went to meet your grandma which i didn't knew was your grandma"

"Wha- you? Wait i don't understand"

I explained him all about how i met her and how i found out it was his grandma

"Wow that is....wow"

I chuckle "i know right"

"Lex"

"Harry"

"Are you gonna go with me? Tomorrow night, for dinner"

I grinned "i would love that"

"Great then i'll pick you up at 8"

"Sure" i smiled but he couldn't see me

"And a dress is gonna be deliver to you at evening so make sure you wear it"

"Dress? Harry no-" he cuts me off

"I love you baby byeee"

I sighed "i love you bye"

Lets see how my date goes with my handsome cute smart ass boyfriend

....

Im so sorry for the small chapter guys!!

I promise next chapter is gonna be worth it And its gonna be a surprise
Love y'all

Part 17

A lexa

The dress was delivered

And i was soooooo shocked when i saw the dressIs he really kidding me?

The dress looked expensive and it was really gorgeous

And to be very honest i have never worn dresses like this

I started getting ready I decided to curl my hair today and i did a little makeup not so much I curl my eyelashes and then applied mascara it looked like i have applied lashes but my lashes were naturally long so i didn't need to use that much mascara any howI changed into the dress and twirled to see how it look It was short but i didn't mindI looked sexxy

It was 7:59 and harry must be here any second now I watched the clock it was 8:00 and the bell rang

Punctual ass

I walk to the door carefully cause i was wearing heels

I opened the door and there stood my man

I gasped a little as i took in his presence

He really want to get laid

He was wearing all black Not a suit But he was wearing formalsHis black shirt hugged his muscular chest his biceps clearly showing through his shirts First two buttons undone showing his toned sexy chest

His hair messily combed he looked so hotHis sleeves were rolled up showing his veiny arms and hands

I didn't noticed his left hand had black ring in his pinky finger

His cologne was so addictive And im damn sure i must be drooling by now

My body hummed as it took in his cologne

I looked up in his grey eyes that were busy in roaming down my body I squirmed in his gaze His jaw was sharp that could cut anything He looked up to meet my gaze

"You look.....so..gorgeous" he took a step forward I release a breathe

He cupped my cheeks and leaned down to kiss me Just as his lips met mine my body was getting hot His warm hand snaked on my waist holding me tightly against himI wasn't able to think as i bring my hand up around his neck to bring him more closer His hand that was on my waist leaned down to settle on my hips he squeezed my hips making me gasp in his mouthHis tongue slide in my mouth He tasted so deliciousWe break the kiss to breathe and he leaned his forehead with mine

He looked in my eye so many emotions swirling in his eyes i don't know what to say

"How do i get so lucky?" He whispered

I frown at him not understanding what is he saying "W-what" i mumble

He bit his lip and released it a second later "you came in my life, i have you what more could i ask for baby?" He mumbled

Okay he really wants me to cry

I pout "i love you" i burry my face in his chest still pouting

My body was loving his warmth his cologne everything about him

He hugged me tightly and leaned his chin on my head "i love you" he say

We get inside his car

Oh he brought Bugatti Chiron That car was wow

The car was filled with his delicious scent

I buckled the seat belt

"Where are we going?" I ask looking at him

His right hand was on steering wheel while the other was on his lap His eyes were focused on the road

He turned towards me and smirk "you'll see"

I nod

He played the song 'Stand by me'

I smiled as i look out of the window

The world seem unreal This seem unreal

I have harry and i am so happy i just.... I am really happy

'Just as long as you stand.... Stand by me'

I look at harry and he has a smile on his face as he looks at me and winks i giggle And lean my head back on the seat as we drive through streets

I took out my phone and took harry's picture He looked at me and frown "don't take my pictures"

"Oh shutup" i say

He pouts

I kiss his pouty lips he grins "I think i should pout often then" he say

I shook my head smiling

We reached at some big building

Harry came up to me opening my door and taking my hand i smile and take his hand he kiss the back of my hand and pull me out carefully

With his hands intertwined with me he lead me inside this amazing building

I saw a man walk towards a us he looked around his fourties

"Mr Stewart, glad to see you here" he say

Harry nodded "likewise"

He looked at me "who must be this gorgeous lady"

"She's my girlfriend" harry said sternly he turned towards me "Alexa meet Tony the owner of this restaurant"

I smiled at tony "nice to meet you"

He smiled back

"Sir you are already reserved so let me guide you to your table" tony said and started walking

We followed behind him quietly

I felt harry's hand resting on my hip i held a breathe He leaned down and kissed behind my ear making me gasp a little

I turned my face towards him and glare at him "he'll see us" i whisper

He smirked "oh really?"

I shook my head at him and he teased me

Tony stopped and he showed us our table

Wow

It showed outside view and we were at the top

Our table was covered with bouquet of white roses

I gasped and picked it up i turned towards harry who was smiling at me

I loveee white roses

I hugged him tightly kissing his lips softly "thankyou" i mumble

"Anything for my queen" he say

I grinned

"You two look great together" tony said and we smiled at him "i'll send a waiter rightaway" he said and left

We sat across each other

"The view is breathtaking" i whisper looking outside

"Yeah" he say

I looked at him and he was looking at me with his head slightly tilted i felt heat creeping up my cheeks making me red

"Harry"

"Sweetheart"

I'll curl in the ball

"Why do you asked me to wear this dress? Is there any special occasion, i mean yeah its our first date but so fancy" i chuckle

He took a glass in his hands gulping the wine that was in it his throat blobbing as he gulped the wineI also gulped looking at himHe put the glass and leaned back looking at me carefully "darling you'll know"

I furrow my eyebrows "isn't this the surprise?" I ask looking around

Bringing me to this expensive restaurant

He slightly shook his head

"Then what is? I am curious tell me please"

"Curiosity killed the cat" he smirked

I rolled my eyes groaning

The waiter came and harry ordered i asked him to order for me as i don't know what is the best here

After giving the order to the waiter Harry turned towards me

"If you think that the surprise will be here, in the restaurant then the answer is no" he say intertwining his hands and keeping his chin on it watching me intently with those grey eyes

"Okay okay fine! I am not saying anything about what the surprise is.. i can wait yeah, i can... i can...." I nod my head to myself "can i?" I ask him

He chuckled "you can"

"okay"

The waiter approached us with the food And oh god did he ordered everything that was on the menu?

Just as the waiter left i turned towards harry "did you just ordered everything that was on menu?" I raise both my eyebrows

"No, i didn't" he place the napkin on his lap and held fork and spoon in his hand his eyes met mine "eat"

I inhale through my mouth and dig in the food

...

No we were done with our food And it was delicious everything in it

"The food was" i put fingers on my mouth and kiss it "amazing"

He nods "yeah i come here often"

"Oh do you?"

"Yes.."

He already payed but we were still sitting "So... shall we?" I ask

"No wait" he say

I frown

A waiter came with the dish in his hand but it was covered i couldn't see what was inside he placed it infront of me and left

"What is it" i look at harry who was acting innocent

He shrug and smiled

I open it and squeal with excitement "donuts??" I grin

There were chocolate donuts in this plate

"Harry you are so getting laid" i say giving him the eye

He grinned showing his perfect teeth"Eat up"

I dig in my donuts shamelessly eating them harry just watched me with awe like i was a hero or someone

He just has a little smile on his face as he watched me

...

We sat in his car again and this time he blindfolded me

Ohhkayyyyy

I didn't asked anything to harry

I bit my lip as harry drive silentlyI felt his thumb on my bottom lip pulling away from my lip"Don't bite your lip or i won't be able to drive" he whisper

I lick my lip and nodded

After 5 minutes we reached

I felt harry getting our of car closing the door he opened my door and helped me out my eyes were still blindfolded

"Harry i'll get blind if you don't open my blindfold" i mumble

I hear him chuckling

He rest one of his hand on my the small of my back and the other hand holding my right hand

"Here we are" he whispered in my ear

He slowly took off my blindfold and i blink first to adjust light

We were at the beach I gasp and my eyes widened

My eyes started to tear up as i saw what was written there

Will you Marry me?

Oh god

This must be a dream

I saw harry sink down on his one kneeHe held one of my hand as i watch him my heart was so full

"Alexa, when you came into my life you made me feel so different.. whenever i used to see you or whenever i used to meet you my heart would do some weird shit." I chuckle as more tears came down my eyes "i used to say this is weird so i ignored it... but for how long? You made me a better person i was a shitty bastard which i am still now, but not for you.. i have been so cold towards you when you expressed your love to me i didn't know what to do because i was feeling the same way but i was afraid i could hurt you... so i left you then i realised i am nothing without you i am a lost person i dont see light when you're not in my life... Alexa i want to wake up and see you laying beside me everyday when i come back home exhausted i wanna see your face that could release all my stress.. i want to have babies with you, i want to grow old with you.. i want to spend each of my happy moment sad moment every moment with you... i want you there by myside holding my hand.. I love you Lex, will you be the only reason of my happiness and will you marry me?" He finishes

And my eyes were hurting with so much tears that fall down like hecking niagra falls

"Yes! Yes... oh my god... harry yes million time yes i will marry you" i say as i cry

He puts out a ring and pushes it on my finger and kisses my hand

Then he stood up wiped my tears and slammed his lips with mine pushing our bodies together It felt like a bunch of butterflies made their way in my stomachHe moved his lips softly against mine and bit my bottom lip

I heard cheering and applause and fire works we back off from kiss and then i saw so many people surrounding us

"Look" harry whisper and points towards the sky

There was a big firework and 'Congratulations!' was written on it

I grinned at it then i looked at harry and saw him looking at me with a soft smile on his lips

I look around the people and i saw grandma standing there clapping

I grinned at her and rushed towards her i hugged her tightly "grandma!" I say

"Congratulations! Honey" she say kissing my forehead i smiled at her

Harry stood beside me grandma hugged him and congratulated him to which he smiled kindly

"Congratulations son" a voice came from behind

I saw a handsome man he looked in his fifties or forties he looked like a businessman.. harry looked like his father his father was also gorgeous but not more than harry, nuh uh

Then there was a lady beside her who had blonde hair she was wearing a dress that showed her breasts alot and her face didn't looked like harry and she was definitely his stepmother

"Thanks father" harry said shoving his hands in his pocket and one hand around my waist pulling me close

Harry's father turned towards me "you are really marrying this bastard huh?" He asked the lady beside her smirked i just blinked at them "well let me tell you in advance he is a cruel heartless person and he will hurt you just like he did to others" he said it and glanced one more time at harry who was glaring at the floor then his father left

I turned towards harry and his hands were in fist by his side his eyes filled with anger and rage

I cupped his cheek "hey...look at me" i say softly

He looked at me and his eyes were red Bloodshot red i gasped

"Harry.. he is stupid he doesn't know you he is just an idiot. I am marrying you that is my decision and you are perfect you are the best person... i love you so much and i willNever leave you and he is lying you would never hurt me i know that" i mumble softly at him caressing his cheek

He didn't say anything just looked at me his eyes were glossy by now

"Come here" i whisper as i wrap my arm around himHe burry his face in my neck releasing a harsh breatheI run a hand through his hair "its okay.." i whisper and i kiss his side face

He looked at me and leaned his forehead with mine "you bring out the best in me, i love you and will never stop loving you until the day i die." He say

Then i keep a finger on his lips and shook my head lightly "don't talk about you dying i don't like it" i mumble

He smiles softly at me and hugged me

I love every second of this life

I love it

....

Crying sobbing throwing up turning in a ballAwwwwwI am so happy for my couple!

I hope this chapter was worth it

I cant wait when their wedding day comes!! I am too excited □□ I hope you like my story till now if you do dont forget to vote comment and share this with your friends Love y'all

Part 18

Alexa

After the proposal harry took me home as i got tired And he stayed

After 2 weeks i will be Mrs Stewart

Oh goddddddd

I do not meet harry often because he is busy with his work He said he is covering up some work because after our wedding we'll be heading for honeymoon and that is why he need to do some work

Logan and i have became really great friends he drops me home because harry is busy, harry asked him to drop me home daily from work

Jack has been nicer to me and that is quiet weird to me but i like this side of him And as for george he is not coming to work jack said he have taken a leave for 10 days he had to visit his parents and family who lives in paris So for now jack has hired a new chef John he is a nice cook and a nice person

(Sorry to disturb your reading but guys i will be skipping to 2 days before wedding when george has return from his home and alexa has already bought her wedding dress with grandma... Continue reading love y'all)

—————-I asked harry to come with me at my work because after harry beat george he haven't seen him and well i invited george at my wedding so it won't be nice if they got in stupid argument or fight

So i am taking him with me to apologise to george which he doesn't know yet

"Why am i going with you?" Harry asked umpteenth time now while driving he shake his head

"I said i will tell you harry have some patience" i say

"Well i don't have any patience" he looks at me more like glare and then back at road

"Don't you dare glare at me or i won't marry you" i say folding my arms

I know i was lying it was just to scare him

He frowns at me still glaring

"I said don't" i grit my teeth

He pursue his lips shaking his head "okay" he mutter

I roll my eyes at him

We are arguing with each other like we are not marrying each other after 2 days

Yeah 2 days!!I am so excited and nervous at the same time

The car comes to a stop and harry parked it

We get off the car and i hold his hand stopping him from going inside

He frowns "what? We aren't going inside?"

I shake my head "listen to me carefully"

"I am all ears" he smiles forcefully

I sigh "when we go inside and when you meet george you have to say 'i am sorry george i said all those things to you and i beat you which i shouldn't have' and apologise nicely" i tell him with my warning voice

"You are shitting me" he said his mouth agape a little

"No, my parents taught me to shit in bathroom" i blurted

He made a disgusting face

"Forget what i said" i say "now lets go inside and you have to say this or i won't marry you"

He groans "why the hell are you bringing marriage in everything. Fine! I will apologise" his nose scrunched up in annoyance

Which i find cute very cute

I smile and kiss his nose

He leans down to my ear level "you have to be careful, because you'll pay for that" he whispers in my ear nibbling my ear I gasp He backed off smirking

Annoying ass

We get inside and george was there

"Hi lexi" he say i smile at him

George looked at harry and froze

I nudged harry

"Uh well hi" harry say to george

Okay this is awkward

"H-hi" george said

"Look what i did was not good and im sorry for that so we're cool?" Harry ask george raising his eyebrows

Such a small apology Well atleast he apologised

"Yeah man" george said and they gave each other bro hug

"Make sure you come at our wedding" harry said patting his back

He coughs "y-yeah sure sure" he smiled"uh excuse me i have work to-" i cut him off

"Yeah sure you can go"

I turned towards harry "that was good"

He cocked an eyebrow "really?"

"Mhm"

"You remember you have to pay right?" He leaned closer "two days" he whispered pecking my lips

"Yeah i know" i bit my lip

He smirked "good"

....

Sorry for the short chapter guys But next chapter will be big and it will include SMUT so i have to write it all and it will take a little timeBut i promise i will upload it as soon as i can

LOVE Y'ALL

Part 19

AUTHORS NOTE

This is NOT the CHAPTER this is the note to you all that from now on my chapters will include SMUT and i will warn you if it comes

It won't be in every chapter but in most of them

And the story haven't finished.. there is a lot still

So i hope you love reading my story till now i have tried my best to write these chapters and if any part disappoints you then i am really sorry I will try my best to not disappoint you!

KEEP READING   LOVE Y'ALL

Part 20

A lexa

This is it...

Its my wedding day...

And i have been crying since morning i don't know im so emotional.. it just..feels like a dream to me a best dream which will finish any time now and i will wake upAnd hell i dont wanna wake up

grandma has been with me and im all ready all set to go there and say my vows to that man and return with him being mine

Its like im going on a war Loll

No lols anymore im emotional

I wipe my tear with my tissue as grandma holds my hand looking at me with sad expression

"Its okay honey.. it happens i know there are mixed feelings coming to you but don't cry anymore honey everything is gonna be perfect" she says softly caressing my hand

I nodded sniffing "yeah" i say my voice barely audible

"Now come on they are waiting we have to go" she said

"Grandma can i please have a minute to myself?" I ask her

She nods completely understanding me "sure honey i'll be right outside"
She gets up and leaves the room closing the door

I started crying again my chest shaking a little as i cry

I wipe my eyes carefully not to ruin my makeup

"Oh god..." i whisper

I sniff "dad i am marrying harry today.. and i am so happy" i pursue my lips
as more tears form in my eyes "i miss you dad.." my voice breaking as i nod
"i really really miss you... i will miss the way u would look at me when u
see me in this dress i will miss the way you would hug me" my chest shake
a little as i cry softly "i hope you're happy dad because i am" i wipe my eyes
last time sighing

"You can do this" i whisper to myself

I look in the mirror last time and i look really gorgeous today

I wore the white long dress that fits me like a glove and shows my curves
but is covered And there is a headcover that is really long

My makeup is nicely done and my hair is up in a beautiful bun there are
two strands of my hair that are infront of my eyes

I close my eyes and sigh one more time

Then i carefully hold my dress and walk outside and i saw grandma she
smiles at me

"Lets go darling" she say i nod smiling a little at her

She holds my arm and then we walk down the aisle i look up and saw harry there

My all worries go away

He was standing there wearing a black tuxedo it made him look very handsome white crisp shirt beneath his black suitjacket his hair styled nicely and slick back his tuxedo hugs his muscular arms and chest his grey beautiful eyes focused on me as he took in my presence his cheekbones were defined his concrete jaw looking so hot his face was glowing he looked like a total model his eyes widen a little and he looked at me with awe

When i reached there his warm hand took mine and he smiled at me this looked magical i smiled back at him he kissed my hand and helped me up

He didn't left my hand instead he held the another one too he looked at me in the eye and i lost in his eyes so deep like he wanted to say so much and his eyes were speaking to me

The priest gives his speech as me and harry still looked at each other likee have never met before

"You're so beautiful i love you" he mouthed to me

I blush "you're very handsome and i love you too" i say mouthing at him he grins showing his white pearly teeths

"Mr harry you should start by saying your vows" the priest says harry nodded at him then his eyes found mine

"Alexa, you are my world my happiness my only light, i promise to be with you in hard times and in good times.. i promise to never make you cry for the tears that will shed from your eye will be the tears of joy, i will be with you in your heart and keep you safe in mine... i will protect you from everything and will never let anything harm you i promise to give you love honesty trust commitment... and keep your life interesting and fun until we grow old. I love you infinity.." Harry finishes his vows and a tear shed from my eye he wipe it away with his thumb shaking his head a little

The priest turns to me "its your turn now Ms Alexa"

I nod and take a breathe "Harry.." i start and harry looks at me intently with soft expression on his face "in your arms, i have found home.. in your eyes i have found love... when you are with me i feel like i am safe.. i promise to stand with you against your trouble.. i promise to never leave you in hard times.. when things go wrong i'll be by yourside holding you..i will love you faithfully and unconditionally through difficult and easy times.. when you need a friend i will be your bestfriend, when you need a help i will be there for you.. when you need care i will support you..i want to grow old with me.. i love you now and forever" i finishes as i saw harry's eyes shine and he smiles at me

A tear escapes from his eye that breaks my heart i quickly move forward and wipe his tear

The priest ask us to say it after him

"I Harry stewart take you Alexa daniels to be my wife,to have and to hold, from this day forward, for better for worse, for richer for poorer, in sickness and in health, to love and cherish always" harry slips a ring in my hand

"I Alexa Daniels take you Harry Stewart to be my husband, to have and to hold, from this day forward, for better for worse, for richer for poorer, in sickness and in health, to love and cherish always" i slip a ring in his hand

And grins at him while he grins at me

"I now pronounce you Man and wife you may now kiss the bride" priest said

Harry bring his arm around my waist and bring me close to him his familiar delicious cologne filled my nose bringing pleasure to my heart then his lips touched mine my hands automatically went around his neck bringing him impossibly close my heart pounded in my chest as my knees got weaker when he move his lips slowly against mine i could only think about how soft his lips are.. then we parted our lips away breathing heavily

"We did it" harry whispered i smiled

Then we turned towards our guest who were cheering loudly

Me and harry walk down the aisle my arms secured around his muscular arm

We smile at our guests..

...

Now it was time for me and harry's slow dance

Harry took my hand and lead me to dance floor They put soft music on and dimmed the lightsThe only lights were on us

I brought my arms up and secured it around his neck he bring his arms around my waist holding me against him We swayed at the music our forehead pressed to each other as we move slowly

Harry twirled me around and i giggle he smiled at me then he brought me closer to him again holding against him like he wanted to tell me he didn't want to let me go

After our slow dance he kissed my lips and everyone cheered applauding

It was now time for dinner

We seated on our table harry beside me and harry's father and his step-mother across usHarry's grandma next to harry

Harry didn't danced with his stepmother The only dance that happened was mine and harry's otherwise it was the relatives of harry that danced

"You are married now harry.. i think you should be a man now start to think and act like a man" his dad said in low voice

He had one arm around his wife and one was holding glass full of champagne

What is wrong with him

"You don't have anything to say huh?" His dad said again

Harry glared at the table and everyone was quiet

I move my hand to his and i carefully intertwined my fingers with him squeezing it a little

His expressions calm downed

I looked at his dad "Mr Stewart i am his wife now and i wont take any disrespect for my husband even if it comes from his father.. kindly respect him and our marriage.. give him some love which i know you would never but atleast be ashamed a little we just got married.. please" i say sternly at him making eye contact with him

His dad narrowed his eyes but didn't said anything

I looked at harry and he was looking at me with awe and shock i squeezed his hands again telling him im there for him he squeezed it back kissing my hand his eyes still on mine

This is it i will not let anyone hurt him more

They have to deal with me before they deal with him

We reached his home but this was not the one he took me in I have never seen this house before

Harry helped me out of the car and i saw this was a big mansion a huge mansion

"Harry this-" he cuts me off

"This is our new home.. i bought this for us" he whispers

I look up at him and hugged him "i love you"

"I love you more my sweetheart" he say

He took my hand and we went inside his house

This house was black and grey themed on the inside

It was more massive then the house he was in

He waste no time leading me towards the elevator

The elevator closed and harry's lips were on mine he softly moved his lips around mine teasing with his tongue my breathing got heavy as he kissed me so lovingly I backed off from kiss "harry we're almost there.. wait a little" i whisper biting my lip

He growls "i can't"

I smile at him

He lead me to his- our room and i was speechless

The room was really huge it was black themed The bed was decorated with white flowers around it

I heard harry close the door and lock it

My heart pounded in my chest as i feel him now just right behind me

"You know how much i have waited for this" he whispered in my ear his two fingers roaming down my cold arm i shiver a little

His hands come down to my waist then settle on my hips His mouth claimed my neck softly kissing there as i whimper he held me firmly against him I leaned my head back on his shoulder move my neck to give him some more access

.....

I am so sorry for the cliffhangerr

But next chapter will be haha

Okayy just a little longer and the chapter will be up!

Keep showering ur love□

Part 21

(18+ VIEWERS AHEAD) MATURE SCENES

THIS IS ONE BIG ASS OF A CHAPTER

Alexa

Harry step back and i look at him He removed his suitjacket throwing it on the arm chair, the muscles in his forearms flexing

He looked at me his eyes burning with hunger then he stalked towards me slowly

I hold a hand up to stop him he stopped and frowns

"Let me change" i say

He groans sitting back on back

I chuckle looking at him acting like a child

I went inside the bathroomChanging in my black nightdressAnd my ass is showing in it not fully

I wipe my makeup faster cause i know harry would be really impatient by now I let my hair down then i slowly twisted the bathroom door knob opening it i get inside the room softly closing the back door

I saw harry sitting on bed his shirt was off and he was now in his black trousers

His muscles perfectly defined as he lay on bed his head leaned back and his eyes closed

I slowly walk there up to him and straddled his lap his eyes shot open and he looked at me then down seeing i straddled his lap

He smirked then he cupped one of cheeks bringing me down to him kissing me softly we moved our lips together in sync i place my hand on his chest feeling him my chest was pressed against his now our kiss turned more urgent as he flips us in one swift motion without breaking kiss i squeal against his mouth

He was the one to back out from kiss "we need to get you out of this" he whispered huskily looking down at my nightsuit

I bit my lip "then remove it"

He licked his lips kissing me again then his hands went down to the hem of my shirt he removed it with one swift motion he removed my shorts

And i was left in my undergarments His warm hand went on my back his cold ring hit my back making me shiver he unclipped it like he was expert in it i gasped that how fast he did itHe smirked tilting his head back to look at me in the eye Then his eyes went down at my breast and his eyes darkened with hunger

"So fucking perfect" he whispered and took my right breast in his warm hand kneading it a soft moan escape my lipsHis mouth found my left breast teasing nipple with his tongue my eyes closed and soft moans escaped my lips He twist and turn my left nipple teasing it

then his hands went down to my underwear he yanked it away i gasped "harry!"

He chuckled sexily

He left kisses down my stomach then his head went to my thigh he kissed there i gasp slowly he kissed further way in

"Look at me" i heard his husky deep voice i opened my eyes looking down at him

He pressed his thumb on my clit making me gasp loudly he massage it in circular motion i moaned in pleasure

"So fucking wet already baby" he whispered

Baby

He removed his thumb and parted my legs more wide, my eyes widen Then his tongue teased my clit i whimper He started eating me there sucking it i moan loudlyAfter some time i came with my body shaking

He looked up at me and i met his hungry gaze my come dripping from his chin he wiped it away with his back of the hand

"I can eat you all day so fucking sweet" he said his voice more deep

I bit my lip

Okay hot ass person

He slowly enter his small finger inside and i gasp biting my lip tightly It was hurting He didn't move his finger he just kept it still watching my expression carefully

"Are you okay? How does it feel?" He ask softly

I lick my lips "it....feels weird its hurting and burning a little"

He nods in understanding "it'll get better.. im sorry for hurting you.." he kissed my knee

I shook my head "no.. you're not hurting me"

He removed his finger from there

"I'll enter my middle finger now okay?"

I gulped nodding slightly

To be honest i was scared cause i have never even touched myself ever

He slowly entered his middle finger and i moan in pain loudly

I shut my eyes tightly gripping the bed cover

"Don't move don't move.." i say with scared voice

"I won't sweetheart" he said softly

He kissed my inner thigh again and again to distract me

"You're so tight" he whispered

He didn't moved his finger

I release a breathe "move your finger a little" i say

He nods slowly then he slowly moves his finger in and out and it was paining but in a good way

I moan slowly as he moves his finger slowly "faster" i pant

"faster?" He asks again

I nod

He started moving faster and i moan as his mouth start eating me out there more moans escaped from my mouth in pleasure

"I...i can't.." i pant

"come for me...do it." His voice demanding

I heard him and then i came all over his finger "harry" moaning his name

This was the second time i came

"I need to widen you.." he said

I bit inside of my cheek gulping i nod

He entered his middle finger then he entered another finger i let out a slow cry

It was paining a lot

After i told him to move he slowly moved his finger

"When you'll about to come tell me" he whisper

I nod not knowing how to speak

After some time i say "im about to.."

He removed his finger and my eyes widen i looked at him with a frustrated frown

He chuckled then he quickly removed his trouser his cock jerked out i gulped looking at the length and it was thick

But i wanted to touch him

My hands slowly went there but he stopped me gripping my wrist softly

"Not today" he said

"Okay.." i reply quietly a little disappointed

What the hell

"You took the pill i asked you to?" He asked

I nodded he nod back

Harry gave me pill that was for birth control

Then he hovered over me balancing his weight on his hand

The strands of his light brown hair falling on his forehead making him look more handsome and cute yeah cute

"I am about to enter okay?" He say his tone soft

"Okay.." i nod

He kissed my forehead then my lips softly

His tip entered my pussy and i gasp

He pecked me thenHe slowly pushed himself inside and i cry out loudly shutting my eyes tightly burrying my face in harry's neck tightly holding him

It was like someone tore me off

"Hey... its okay its okay..." he whispered Kissing my head "it'll be okay... i am not moving okay? Im so sorry for hurting you.." he kissed my shoulder

He wasn't doing it on purpose!!

I wanted to say it to him but i was in too much pain so i just whimper

"You're so beautiful.. so fucking perfect.. my lex" he whispered in my ear softly

Trying to distract me and i did got distracted a little for how softly and how fondly he was saying it like he really mean it

Tears escaped my eyes for how much it was hurting

"You're soo tight baby.." he say

I whimper

He stayed still without moving "shh its okay its okay.." he comforted me again softly caressing my hair

I burried my face in his neck so tightly

Somehow it was comforting me his warmth his closeness

I looked up at him and his eyes were closed and his mouth opened a little

Like he was enjoying it it was pleasuring him

"Are you having pleasure?" I ask him

He looked at me his eyes half opened looking like he's drunk "you feel so fucking good"

He leaned down and started kissing me softly.. moving his lips in sync with mine my hand went upto his hair playing with it softly tugging it

He didn't move just kissed me

After kissing for what felt like and eternity my muscles loose around his cock

"You can move..." i say quietly

"okay.." he replied softly

Then he kissed my forehead and my nose

He started moving slowly i hissed with pain he stopped "shit.. im so sorry i am so sorry baby.." he kissed my cheek and my lips

I shook my head "no.. just keep going" i say

I knew he needed to come too so i asked him to move

"Are you sure baby?" He asked in soft tone again his voice sad and concerned

I nodded "yes just keep moving..but slow"

He nods again

I pressed my lips tightly as he thrusted as slowly as he can at first it was hurting but then

I started to get pleasure as i moan loving his skin against mine

I bring his head down so i could kiss him I kissed his mouth when he thrusted inside me

"Faster...faster" i pant

He started moving faster and our pants and moans filled the room The sound of our bodies colliding filled the rooms His thumb found my clit and he rubbed there in circle thrusting inside me he groans and My eyes roll back in pleasure as i let out a moan

"Your pussy love my cock" he whisper in my ear and i moan at how he dirty talked to me

I loved it

"Your tight little pussy only belongs to my cock..and my cock only belongs to you.." he whispered

And i found it somewhat funny how dirty he is talking so i chuckled but it was replaced with a moan when he thrusted in me deep

After some time me and harry came together and he filled me with his hot seeds

He removed his cock and i saw blood all over it my eyes widened He took the tissue from side table and wiped himself then he took towel and wiped me carefully i looked at him with awe

I thought we were done

Keyword: thought

Then he flipped us and now he was lying down and i was straddling his lapHis cock on my thigh now

He smiled at me his grey eyes dark and filled with hunger but one thing that was more filled was, love....he started sucking my breast i moaned and pushed my breast more further in his mouth shamelesslyHe teasingly bit my nipple and i gasp and whimper

Then his hands hold my arm and he pulled me up

And his tip was at my clit ready to go in

"Come on... ride me" he say tilting his head like he didn't know what to do

I kept eye contact with him as i held his shoulder for supportI slowly slide down moaning

He was feeling more bigger in this position

And then i heard him moan and that was the sexiest thing i ever heard

It was like heaven to my ears

I started to move up and down and my breast bounced as i move he growls and i moan

I looked at him and his eyes slightly opened and he was biting his lip he looked so fucking sexy watching me ride him he looked at my breast and started kneading it pinching my nipple playfully

My body hummed in pleasure as my heart pounded in my chest

He looked so immensely gorgeous and sexy aa his hair sticked to his forehead with sweat on his forehead making him look more hot then he is

"Yeah..just like that....fuck" he pant he growls lowly"Ride my cock like a good girl.." he whispered pushing my hair back that was coming infront of my eyes

I bit my lip and my eyes roll back "yes!"

"I am close come for me... baby" he whispered licking his lips

And i obeyed him and came with him and he filled me with his seeds...again

We pant together as he was still inside me he slowly moved back and forth and i moaned then i leaned on him my breast pushed against his chest my hands around his neck

He slowly removed himself from me and i felt empty

He kissed my head

"That was.....magical" i say

He hummed "it was magical"I looked up at him and he was smiling i smiled back at him

"I'll be back" he whispered and slowly removed me from him kissing my lip softly then he disappeared in washroom

I look down and our bedsheet was red with my blood i gulped

He came back with boxers on

He came up to me and picked me up in his arms i just watched his gorgeous face his grey eyes that was staring ahead

How could someone be so damn perfect

We went inside the bathroomHe softly placed me on the counter he took the towel and open the faucet making it a little wet then he wiped me off softly like he was scared to hurt me

I just watched him with love

I am so in love with this man

When he was done he looked up at me and smiled at me

He pressed his forehead with mine looking at me with more love "I love you" he whispered

I smiled softly at him "i love you too"

The night..the day was perfect

.....

Here goesss there first night!

They did it... my babies have grown up!

Please vote comment□

LOVE Y'ALL

Part 22

Harry

I woke up blinking 2 3 times I turned around but i felt warmth and soft snores

I look down and i saw alexa her face buried in my neck her hair all over her face and her hand around my torso her one leg around my leg hugging me tightly against her

I smiled at her

She is so gorgeous so innocent I don't know how someone like me can deserve someone like her?She is too good to be true

I look at her softly pushing the strands of her hair back from her head carefully so i don't wake her up

I softly pressed my lips on her forehead then keeping my chin on her head closing my eyes

I felt lex move a little then she looked up at me her beautiful blue eyes looking at me

And she smiled more like blushed for what we did last night

I smirked at her winking

She buried her face in my chest not showing her face to me

I chuckled burying my face in her hair "you felt so good" i murmur in her hair

"Shutup harry!" She buried her face more in my chest

I chuckle "what?"

"Don't say that.. i am just..." she look up at me and she was red with all the blush she bit her lip "its new to me and i..." i cut her off

"I know i was just teasing you.. i am sorry" i say pouting a little

She grinned and softly pressed her lips to mine she wanted to move but i cupped her cheeks kissing her back

I kissed her fighting for dominance she kissed me back with same dominance then i gave in and she smiled in the kiss and pushed her tongue inside my mouth now kissing me softly

I flipped us around and now her tiny body laid under me

I smirked at her as she looked at me with that fucking doe eyes

My cock twitched with pain

I leaned down and kissed her she cupped my face but i took both of her hand and pushed it above her head with my one hand i bit her lip sucking it softly

I move down and started kissing and sucking her neck she moan.. fucking hell

My cock jerked in interest

I pressed my forehead with her as she release soft breaths

"You wanted to touch me yesterday" i whisper

She nodded "C-can i touch you now?" She asked with those doe eyes

I bit my lip "fuckk" i kissed her with hunger pushing my tongue inside her mouth "touch me" i whisper in her mouth

I sit up beside her then she straddled my lap i smirked

Her eyes went down to my cock and she bit her lip

She moved her soft hand and wrapped around my cock

I growl

She started moving her hand up and down softly

"Grip it tightly" i pant looking at her she nod

She gripped only a little tight

I gripped her hand that was wrapped around my cock "look" i say

I grip her hand tightly then i started moving up and down with more pressure

She look at me with sad expression "i will hurt you"

My heart broke for how softly she said it

I cupped one of her cheeks "hey...baby you ain't gonna hurt me okay?" She nods biting her lip i brought her face closer to me and kissed her while she move her hand up and down with pressure

I moan a little and she looked at me with hunger

"I love how you moan" she whisper

I grinned "yeah?"

"Mhm"

My head fall back with pleasure at how her soft hands held my cock

"Baby... i am about to" i was gonna finish my sentence when her tongue started teasing my cock

"Fuckk" i grabbed the back of her head tugging it

"Yeah keep looking at me with that beautiful blue eyes" i say

She started taking me in her mouth i gasp

She started moving her head up and down my cock

Then i came and she swallowed my come some of my come dripped from her chin

"You're so hot" i whisper huskily

She smirked

I caressed her cheek "I loved how you swallowed my come..." she bit her lip

"Was it okay with you?" She ask

"More than fucking okay.." i say she giggled and i grinned

She started getting up

I stopped her "where do you think you are going? I haven't even started yet"

Her eyes widen then it rolled in pleasure when i thrusted inside her

.....

Alexa

Me and harry having sex was like i am in heaven

The way he fucks me it is soo pleasurable

The fact i was sore but i still wanted him inside of me

And he made me come many times

I loved how he was enjoying me sucking his cock or me wrapping my hand around his manhood

His expressions gave it all for how much pleasure i was giving him and i loved it

I was turning shameless

God forgive us

After taking shower i went down to where the kitchen was

The breakfast was already ready and it was on dining table

So i didn't went inside kitchen instead i sat down on the dining table waiting for harry to come down

He came down looking so fuckable

Alexa!! You need to calm your hormones down you just had sex!

I don't knoww i wanna do it again

What the-

I gulped as i took in his presence

His hair wet from shower but well brushed still some of his strands fall down on forehead

He was wearing dark blue suit following with dark blue button down shirt, first two buttons undone showing his toned chest and his suit hugged his muscular chest and muscular arms he was wearing rolex watch that he always wears and that i don't know why make him looks so attractive

His jawline sharp his eyes found me and his features softened he smiled at me i smiled back at him

He came and sat beside me on the head of the dining table

He leaned down and kissed me softly

"You look beautiful" he say

"Thankyou.. and you look eatable" i nod at myself

He chuckled i grinned biting my lip

He took the bacon bread and egg and placed it on my plate

I frown at him "wha-" he cut me off

"Come on be a good girl and eat" he say

I was too stunned to speak

I wait for him to fill his plate

He started eating then i started eating too

We chatted about random stuff

"Whats your dream place to visit?" Harry ask as he munch on bacon

"London, switzerland.. there are alot of places why?"

He shrugs "just asking"

I hummed in response

He finished eating wiped his mouth and he stood up he looked at his watch "okay i gotta go i'll be back before you know it" he kissed me softly

I cupped his face to keep kissing him

I can't help myself his kisses are sweet and addictive

I backed from kiss pressing my forehead with him "don't go" i mumble

He smiles and cup my cheek "i'll be back soon baby i promise okay?" He says softly

I nodded like a child "okay"

He kissed me again and hugged me tightly i buried my face in his chest inhaling his cologne

God his cologne... my mouth start watering

He kissed my head "i love you bye.." he says

"I love you too bye bye" i wave him he smiles last time and disappeared outside

I was sad Really sad because he left for work

Why was i too attached to him?

I just wanted to be clingy and hold him forever and never let him leave

....

HIIIII GUYSSS

How was the chapter ??

I hope you liked the chapterPlease vote comment

LOVE Y'ALL

Part 23

A lexa

Sometimes i think life is a dream, considering by the fact i am so happy nowadays it feels like my dreams are fulfilled, i always wanted to marry someone i love and i did, i always wanted to have sex with someone who i love and i did!

Harry was right when he said he'll be back before i know it

He was back in two hours

Now we were packing

Harry just announced that we are leaving for honeymoon and i got so happy that i hugged him and stayed there like a koala and he didn't seem to hate koalas by the fact that he was holding me for long time, it looked like he loved koalas.... or Me

He didn't told me where we are going and i didn't bother asking anyway

"For how long are we going?" I ask him as i zip the suitcase that i just packed

"I am not quite sure, how long do you want it to be?" He tilt his head, his hair looking like he have brushed his fingers through them alot of time

I bit my inside cheek "a month? That would be a lot right"

He scowls "what? No. Dominic, one of my business partner.. he went for 3 months" he shrug casually

My eyes widen "don't he have work to do?"

"He have many assistants and workers behind him, and so do i but i don't want any workloads on them" he states truthfully

I smile at his kindness

"When did he married?" I ask getting curious

"A year ago? I don't know.. he did arrange marriage" he sips his coffee

"Arrange marriage? And still they went for 3 months. Impressive" i say nodding

He nod "yeah"

Our packing was done..

I wonder where harry is taking me, but i will be happy as long as he is by my side

Harry stood up as he glances at his watch "we have to leave in 20 minutes" he look up at me "do you need to freshen up?"

I shake my head lightly "no i already did"

He removes his watch and suit jacket "guess i need to do it" as he rolls his sleeves up and his veiny and muscular forearms and arms came in view I gulp at the sight "okay" i say quietly

He looks at me for a minute then he stride towards me

He stood only a few inches far and my body was still heating up

I gulp as he leaned down "will you join me?" He whisper

"I don't shower with chimpanzee.. oops sorry" i tease him

He narrow his eyes "back with chimpanzee thing huh?"

He tilt his head lightly and brushed the strands of my hair back my hair "you didn't care when you were loving this chimpanzee's co-" i cut him off

"Harry! For heaven's sake" i felt heat brush my neck and my face and i bet i was fully tomato red by now

He smirked in satisfaction as he saw me blush "do you wanna recall the memory darling?" His tone was soft and it felt like honey but his words were sending heat up my thigh

I clear my throat as i step back while his damn smirk didn't wipe off his face "go shower now"

He licks his bottom lip "you know i'd love if you joined maybe this chimpanzee would show you-" i cut him off

"Go!!!" I bury my face in my hand

That i know i would be so red even tomato would look light then me

I felt him laugh and it felt like warm thing in my chest

His hands touched my shoulder and just his touch reminded me of morning and last night

Somewhere i still needed to recall it

God why didn't i said yes when he asked

"Baby" his voice soft and gentle as his hand caress my hair gently "look at me"

I shook my head

"Please" he said more gently

I finally looked up at me and bit my lip "i know i am a mess" i mumble

He scowls as his expression hardened "who said that to you?"

"Everyone says that" i fiddle with my fingers

His fingers gently held my chin and made me look up to meet his eyes

"Whoever said that give them my number, i'll deal with those fuckers, perhaps the next thing that come out from their mouth will be screams of pain" a cold smile touch his lips that didn't reached his eyes

"Harry" i warn him

"We are not discussing those dicks now" his tone made me shutup

He adds "I was teasing you back then and no you're not a mess you're fucking perfect to me in every way.. got that?" He raise his eyebrows

I nod "yeah"

"Good girl now brighten up your mood we're going for honeymoon you seem to forgot that" he smiles

Slowly a grin spread over my face "yeah! Heck yeah i forgot about that! I am so happy" i squeal and bring him down for a hug

He chuckled as he wrap his strong arms around me tightly

Thats it

Freeze the moment

We were now in harry's private jet

I was too stunned and surprised when he told me he had a private jet !

I mean yeah he is rich but private jet?Holy cow

Harry sat beside me typing something in his phone with a scowl on his face

I lean on his shoulder and he kissed my hair softly to which i smile

I look out of the window as i see we were now up above the sea

I sigh as i think about asking harry about my jobHarry told me to resign the job because he said it isn't good for me? Like come on i have been working here since so long! And how can he just say that-

"You look deep in thought" his voice quiet and gentle

I lean back and look at him while he smiles at me

"I need to ask you about something" i say

He furrow his eyebrows a little "okay.... Is it serious?"

"Yeah but-" he cuts me off

"Sweetheart, save it for later i don't want something like that ruin our honeymoon we'll discuss whatever you're thinking now i promise but after our honeymoon" his thumb softly caress my hand

I nod slowly in agreement

Yeah i also wouldn't like harry's mood i don't want to ruin it. ever

"You're right.. i am sorry i was just thinking about it" i shook my head slowly

"You don't need to apologise, my love.. got that?" He leaned down to kiss my forehead

"Yes" i smile

He leaned down and captured my lips and slow and sensual kiss and that made me forgot about everything.. for now

I will still ask him about all this after our honeymoon

....

What are your favourite parts?

I just love when harry teases alexa !!That is my favourite part

And also where Harry gets possessive

Oh lalaaa

More scenes will be coming up like that!!

Keep showering with your love

I really love y'all!

Part 24

A lexa

The first destination that harry took us to was

Freaking Maldives!

I mean i really wanted to go there since i was 10 years old and i use to dream of going with the love of my life and here i am

I sigh as i look around the island it was beautiful

Harry booked us the island to ourselves i was once again too stunned to speak

Harry was wearing floral button down shirt and he looked handsome in it the first two buttons were as usual undone, and shorts

He wrapped his arms around my waist from the back and i smiled holding his forearms his cologne driving me crazy already

"Do you like it?" He mumble leaning his head on the side of my head

I turn my head back to look in his gorgeous grey eyes that never fail to mesmerise me i cup one of his cheeks caressing it "I love it"

he smiles showing his cute dimples

kill me

I turn around fully and his hands rest on my hip

I bring his head down to kiss him softly

Leaning my forehead with his i sigh "is this really the first destination? How many places are we going to?"

He smirked his eyes lazily watching me "many" he replied

"You aren't gonna tell me are you?" I fold my arms but he was holding me too close to him that my arms were pressed against his hard chest

He shake his head lightly still smirking

"Is there some way i can convince you?" I bit my lip caressing his broad shoulder with my finger softly

My hands went down and grabbed his growing erection

His smirk faded slowly and i smirked internally

Haha bitch

"Alexa.." he warned his face pained

"What? Is there something wrong?" I acted innocent blinking at him

I tightened my hold and he let out a low growl "fucking hell baby... if you keep touching my dick i won't waste no time fucking you here infront of everyone"

I lick my lips "i'll like that"

His eyes burned with hunger and they were darkened he pinned my hand back and he leaned down his mouth just inches away from me "no one sees whats mine" he pinned me more tightly making me jerk "so that little wish of yours cant be fulfilled darling"

"You're boring" i say rolling my eyes

He let go my hand only to hold me tight against him by my waist

"And you're sexy" he winked

I chuckle

I already changed in my bathing suit when i get inside our private suite

Our private honeymoon suite was big ass Harry booked us the largest one

Harry was already outside

I made my way outside and then my mouth fell open for the sight

He was wearing black shorts as he swims in the ocean his hair wet with water sticking to his forehead and his hot half naked body chiselled and toned his abs showing perfectly water dripping down his torso

I gulp blinking at him

I mean is he really the man i married? Are you sure?

Harry saw me and he passed me sly grin then swam towards me

"Hello there hottest chimpanzee alive" i almost whistle at the sight

He was grinning but it faded when i said chimpanzee

"I am not a fucking chimpanzee, come on" he groan

I laughed at the way he was acting "okayyy mr horse face.. how's that" i wiggle my eyebrows

He looked at me with bored expression "seriously? Well okay ursula" he say mocking my way and then he regret saying that within next second

I gasped loudly "What! What did you say?" I narrow my eyes at him as i talk slow steps towards him

His eyes wide "shit. No thats not what i meant i mean-" i cut him off

"Ursula?? Really??" I say in low voice

He looked up at the sky and closed his eyes "god forgive all my sins and please save me from ur- SHIT i mean lex" he murmur the words

I know he is doing it on purpose

"Harry!!" I scream and run towards him

He start running towards the water

"I am gonna kill you!" I yell while running

"God save me! I am gonna DIE" harry yells mocking my tone

I start laughing

I finally caught him or he slowed down

i wrapped my arms around his torso "gotcha!!" I say giggling

"Shit man." He pouted

I started splash water on him he started doing the same

And we laughed doing that

I sat on his back keeping his head inside the water drowning him

And he didn't bother i removed my hand from his head and he stayed inside more

"Harry come out" i say he didn't budge and stayed like that

"Harry...its not a joke" i murmur

No... he didn't move

My eyes widened with horror as i screamed and his head shot up within a second

He gasp for air as he push his hair back "what.." he pant "what happened"

"Oh god.." i mumble hugging him tightly "don't ever do that... you scared me to death" i bury my face in his wet chest

"I was just joking" he say softly running his hand up and down my arm

"Don't do it please" i say quietly

"Okay...got it" he replied kissing my forehead

We get inside showered and changed

Harry intertwined his hands with mine as we walk on the sand bare foot it was night and we could see all the shining stars and beautiful moon from here

The wind blows and it ruffle my hair harry slowly push the hair behind my ear wrapping his arm around my waist bringing me close to him I wrap my arm around his torso

I felt a rock hitting my ankle and i almost fall As harry was holding me i never fall

I bite my lip keeping me from screaming "Ow ow ow ow" i say

"Lex what happened?" Harry asked looking down at my foot worriedly

I pursue my lips as my face pained "i hit a rock owww" i hissed

I glared at the rock "damn you!! Rock you shit face!" Harry bit back a laugh

I groan holding my ankle "it is hurting" i pout looking at harry tears started forming in my eyes one of the tears escaped my eye he quickly wipe it off

Harry kissed my pouty lips and i smile

He kneeled down taking my ankle and kissing it softly where it hurts

He softly caress it and i hiss he stopped

"Want me to pick you up?" He ask

I nodded pouting

"Don't pout or i'll not stop kissing those adorable lips" he said kissing me again

I giggle

I don't want you to

Then he asked me to hop on his back and he gave me a piggy bank rideAnd i held him tight burying my face in his neck smiling

Gosh i love this man

....

AwwwwWhere the hell is my Harry?

Harry and Alexa have my heartttt

They are so cute

I hope you love this chapter I enjoyed writing it!

I LOVE Y'ALL

Part 25

(I skipped honeymoon phase! Because there is still alot of the story left so i skipped it..)

Also this chapter is dedicated to @yamanista she is really supportive and i love you girl!! This chapter is for you

Harry

We're back home.

I took her to her dream places that she told me aboutWe went to Maldives, Switzerland, Mexico, Greece and Paris

She was jumping up and down and she showered my face with her sweet kisses when she saw Eiffel tower

I fucking loved that adorable smile on her face and for that smile i could do anything

I brushed my hair looking at myself last time then i looked at alexa who was soundly sleeping on the bed

I smiled at her then i walk there and sat beside her "Lex" I whisper caressing her cheek she murmured something pouting

Those fucking lips and those fucking pouts gets me everytime

"Baby..i am heading to office" I say kissing her forehead

She opened her eyes and blinked at me then she gave me a lazy smile "Harry?. When will you come back?" Her voice hoarse a little as she ask me quietly

"I have a lot of work to do but i'll try andCome back soon" I softly smile at her

She sits up rubbing her eye then she came on my lap and hugged me tightly

I hugged her back sighing

She bury her face in my neck "come back soon okay.?" Her voice soft and little

I nod kissing her head

She backed off from hug still on my lap she leaned and I smiled then....

she kissed my nose

and i frown at her

"You seem to forget my lips" I point at my lips "are here"

She pursue her lips "morning breath" light pink shade touched her cheek

"I don't give two flying fucks about it" I grabbed her face and kissed the heck out of her she chuckled on my lips making me smile

She taste fucking delicious

After saying goodbye to alexa

I went where the car was parked I sat in the backseat taking my ipad out
And started working on it

My phone vibrated I saw the caller id My secretary, ana

"Ana" I greeted in stern voice

"Sir, good morning" she say nicely

"Morning, i'll be there in 15 minutes, schedule my meetings with Mr.jos
eph and Mr.johnson"

"Noted sir"

I look at my watch "when will you arrive?"

"Sir I am already in the office and..." she stopped

"What ana?" I say

"your father is also here" she blurted

My eyebrows furrow I pinch the bridge of my nose and sighed

I decided not to answer as I hung up

What does he want now?

—

I get inside the elevator pushing the button

The elevator opened and I stepped outside the workers greeted me while I
nodded

When I am in office my work mode is on and I don't smile often I just focus
on my work

I went inside my office and froze

There he was sitting on my chair with one leg on his another and Claire on his lap

My jaw clenched as I glare at him"What are you doing in my office" my voice low

"Harry my son" he laughed while claire smirked. Bitch

I rolled my eyes "fuck off with that son thing, say what you wanna say and get the fuck out of my office" my nose flared as I burn hole in his head

"Respect your father harry" his voice warning me as he glare at me now

I chuckled bitterly "respect? Are you fucking with me right now? Dad" I say the word like its the most disgusting word in the world

His eyes narrow as he lean back "where's your bitch?" He asked and claire laughed

I saw red when he said that my mind wasn't working as My veins popped out and my hands form a tight fist

I storm towards him and grabbed his collar harshly pulling him up jerking claire fell down with a thud "If you called her that again i'll shoot you here right now without a blink" I said gritting my teeth

I pushed him back and he also fell

"Get out of my office" I say running a hand on my face "OUT! BEFORE I KILL YOU!" I yell at himMy body shake with anger

He stood up dusting his pathetic suit "I had a deal for you" he looked at his shoulder toClaire and she smirked winking at me

Ignoring her I ask "What deal?"

Alexa

Today i'll talk to harry about me working

I can't stay caged at home I mean i've been working and i can't just stay at home now

And also jack had offered me to work again and I said i'll think about it and speaking of george he said he'll come to meet me I called him over dinner for tomorrow

He has been my really good friend but he seemed weird when i was around harry and also he left really early on my wedding day I couldn't even meet him Something was off

I showered and changed in jeans and wore cream colour off shoulder top

I cooked the dinner for me and harryHe like grilled chicken alot so I cooked it singing my favourite songs

After cooking dinner I plop down on sofa turning the tv on

I played Tangled watching it Its my favourite movie

I saw the watch and it was 10:30 and harry was still not home

After a while the door banged open and I stood up hurriedly

Harry came inside his suitjacket off and his tie loose his hair was mess, Before I could say anything.. He went upstairs without looking around

I followed him quietly without saying anything he went inside our room slamming the door shutI flinched blinking at the door i hesitantly twisted the knob and went inside the room I shut the door slowly closing it

Harry was nowhere in sight I heard the shower running, I sighed as I keep my phone on the bed stripping off my clothes I went inside the bathroom and I saw him there his head hung low as he take slow breaths

He didn't feel my presence or maybe he don't want me to be here but I can't leave him when he is sad or angry That is the part where he needs me really much

I slowly step inside the shower with him as I run hand on his back slowly kissing him on the shoulder

He sigh "alexa you should sleep" he say as he run his hand on his hair

"No i am here and i am not sleepy" I mumble

I wrap my hands around his torso leaning my cheek on his back "what is it?" I ask

"There's nothing i am just....stressed thats all, work load"

I tilt my head "but you seem sad and angry.. is there something you're hiding from me?"

He shake his head slowly and he doesn't speak anything

WARNING: 18+ CONTENT FURTHER:

I bit my lip and sighed then I walk infront of him

He doesn't meet my eye as his eyes were closed and his head hung low

I cupped his cheek and he opened his eyes looking at me I pressed my forehead with him "what is it" I mumble

He send me a small smile that didn't reached his eyes "there's nothing sweetheart"

I blink at him not saying anything as my eyes went down at his lips

There is one way he could release his stress

I leaned and captured his lips with mine he doesn't move his lips first but Insoftly suck his lip I gasped as he started kissing me with hunger he flipped as and he pushed me at the wet tiles His body pressing with mine as he kissed me with so much in him

Its okay baby

He backed off and breath heavily "I can't have sex right now baby I might hurt you" he says softly

I shake my head "no.. I want you right now"

His cock jerked in interest as i smirked at him "see your cock doesn't mind"

He send me a sly grin "you little vixen" he smashed his lips with mine

His hand went down my thigh "jump" he say his lips still on mine

I jump wrapping my legs around his torso and my hands around his neck

His hot mouth went down my neck kissing and sucking there softly as I gasp and moan softly "harry.." he bit there playfully making me moan loudly

He leans back breathing heavily his chest rose and fell with each breath he takes "I am not gonna do foreplay is it alright?" He says

I nod without thinking he kissed me softly

Then his hand went down to his cock as he guide it to my entrance his tip touched my core and I shiver

He slowly enter inside me making me gasp and moan he growls lowly "fuck" he started moving faster and faster as I loved how he fucked me "Oh my god.." I moan "I fucking love your sweet moans.. moan for me baby" he says in my ear groaning

He fucked me harder as I moan his name shamelessly

A familiar feeling came inside my stomach the pressure was building inside me as I moan "i am about to..." I pant

He sucked my breast without saying anything

I came all over him with a shake We breath heavily our pants filled the washroom

Harry was ready for round two as we did it again and I loved it more than anything

He pressed his wet forehead to mine closing his eyes "i fucking love you" he whisper

I smile as I cup his cheeks he open his eyes and they were filled with love "I love you" I say kissing his lips softly than wrapping arm around his head smashing his head in my breasts and he loved it

We showered together then changed in our nightsuits

"Harry I cooked your favourite" I fiddled with my fingers

He gave me a soft smile his features softened

Phew

"really?" He ask raising his eyebrows a small smile still playing on his lips

I nod smiling back at him

"Okay then what're we doing here lets go and eat" he say standing up

Well mister grumpy ass you were the one who came up without even seeing around

I wanted to say it but I close my eyes and sighed "yeah lets go"

I squealed when he scoop me in his arms picking me up "harry!" I say shocked

He chuckled his chest shake softly

"If you don't know I can walk" I say in bored tone

"Well I am aware of that sweetheart" he kiss my head

"Put.me.down" i say glaring at him

He just looked at front a smile on his lips

"Harry" i almost choked him

"Baby" he say

Okay shutup THIS IS CHEATING!

"Pleaseee" i pout doing my best to show him my puppy eyes

"Okay stop, stop with those adorable fucking pouts" he groan

I smirked

"I am still not putting you down" he kissed my nose

My smirk dropped and i frown at him

I rolled my eyes and sighed as i lay my head on his shoulder now not arguing

....

Hi guys!! I love you all so much, more than you think!

Sorry i took long writing the chapter actually i was busy!I am really sorry!

A big hug to you all □

LOVE Y'ALL

Part 26

A lexa

Harry didn't told me about the stress he was taking, i mean there must be something thats bothering him to the most

I sigh as i fill my glass with juice It was 10 in the morning and harry was already gone with a note saying 'There is important business i need to deal, don't worry i'll be back, eat the breakfast i made for you.. i love you'

I was mad at him i should be mad at him He could've woke me up like that day so i could say goodbye to him

Though i still ate the breakfast he left for me, and boy does he cook well He cooks amazing i don't know if he was the one who cooked it or he door-dashed it

I groan as i look at myself in the mirror I was missing him, his heavy presence his warm rough hands on me his cologne

I called george today and he would be here anytime now i cooked lasagne because its his favouriteI placed the dish on the dining table and looked at the clock it was 1:00pm

The doorbell rang and i went to open the door, i opened it revealing a smiling george

He came to give me a hug but i stepped back, he froze his gaze turning ice then it went away with a flicker, He clear his throat

"C-come inside" i say sweetly

"Uh, yeah" he say awkwardly

Man this is gonna be awkward

I lead him towards the lounge area We sat on the sofa i sat across from him Not wanting to be close I would maintain my distance And he should also know i am married now

"How has everything been?" I ask

He shrug "same, but there's no fun when you're not at the office"

I nod slowly smiling at him "you know, harry doesn't like me working there so i had to..."

"Yeah" he chuckled waving it off "yeah i totally understand that" he say that a light sarcastic tone touching his tongue

I frown a little

What was with him today?

"Anyways, how is jack" i say

He remained silent he looked up at me and there was rage in it, i froze He glared at me "you never asked how was me"

"I- i was about to" i chuckled nervously "h-how are you george" i say getting scared a little but i didn't show him a sweat trickled down my forehead which i wiped away

He closed his eyes releasing a satisfy breath "when you say my name" he muttered

I frown and i stood up "what is wrong with you george?" I say

He glared at me "What is wrong with me? What is wrong with you! God-damnit!" I flinch at his harsh tone

"You never fucking noticed how much i love you!?? Do you? You never fucking saw i loved you more than anything! You were blinded by harry, so fucking in love with him" he yelled while my face was pale and i stood there with shock

He loved me?

My breathing got heavy as i saw him with disapproving look

He run a hand down his face "you know, you're just a fucking slut you saw harry's money and you ran onto him" he said looking at me with disgusting expression

"Geo-" before i could say anything a loud growl came from behind me

my heart dropped.... I knew who it was George's gaze flick behind me at him

I listened his heavy steps coming close as my heart started beating faster and faster

His cologne brushed my skin and he didn't looked at me he brushed from beside me striding towards him pushing george on to the wall

I rushed there not knowing what to say or how to stop him i just saw harry's hard glare on george following with a gun cocked at his forehead

"You were a fucking idiot to say that word to my wife" harry's dangerous tone sent a shiver down my spine, he pressed a gun more tightly to his forehead a blood ran down from there george hissed making my eyes widened

"Harry!" I say but he didn't listened to me

He brought the gun down to his chin "i'll find you and kill you and everyone you love personally, if i saw you within 50 feet near my wife" harry's chest rose and fell with each harsh breath he took

He slapped his head with his gun hard and george made a pain noise "am i clear?" Harry asked gritting his teeth

I know his blood must be boiling by now

Harry took a step back and looked lazily at george, george took a step forward to leave and harry shot him on the knee, george screamed "That's for calling my wife a slut" Harry said "get the fuck out of my house now"

George held his knee and somehow he left

Me and harry stood there, my head was down looking at the ground while i knew harry's gaze was on minethe silent surrounded us neither of us speaking Why did he shot him? Just because he called me a.....

i sighed and started walking

"Lex" he called but i didn't stopped i kept walking I felt him following me

I went inside our room and sat on the bed looking down I felt him come in

"Harry i don't wanna talk right now" i say in low voice

He didn't say anything as he closes the door and came where i sat

He kneeled infront of me i still didn't looked at him

"Look at me" he say

I stayed still not moving not doing anything

His hands came up to cup my cheek i backed off "don't touch me with the blood in your hands" i say my voice shaking

He blinked "okay i'll come in a second" he disappeared in washroom i heard water running for a while it stopped and he came back kneeling again

"Please look at me baby" his voice soft it ache my heart i looked at him and his face was sad he sighed "i shot him because i was ang-" i cut him off

"Don't tell him why you shoot him, just...don't" i shake my head "and why the hell are you carrying a gun with you?" I ask with my eyes widened

"It's mine i carry it...not often" his voice gentle

I scoffed "okay"

"Baby please... i am sorry okay? I shouldn't have" he stopped shaking his head "no i was right shooting him" he finished the anger burned his eyes as he glared at the wall

I frown but then i decided not to argue so i stayed silent

....

OkayyyI am really busy nowadays because of my studies so whenever i got a free time i begin writing so please don't mind it I would try and write as much as i can!

LOVE Y'ALL

Part 27

A lexa

Harry got up on his foot, I glanced up at him and he ran his hand down his faceHis gaze met mine "You know.. I do not regret shooting that bastard" he say his grey eyes were darkened with anger

He scoffed "it would be better if I killed him"

I stood up looking at him with disbelief "why are you like this harry?" I ask quietly

His eyes connect mine and it was no longer set with fire, his gaze was calm "like what alexa?" He spoke

I flinched

He never called me alexa...

I sighed ignoring it "I just.. I...please give me keys of another bedroom" I say not looking in his eyes

He was silent so I looked up and froze, his eyes were filled with sadness and one moreEmotion which i couldn't figure out he blinked and it went away "the doors are opened" he answered and with that he disappeared in washroom shutting the door loudly I flinch

I grabbed my phone and slowly exit our bedroom not wanting to stay with him todayAnd thankfully he didn't argued

Maybe he is tired?Of me?

I shook my thoughts away as I lay on the queen size bed staring up the ceiling The only voice I could hear was of clock ticking and my slow breaths I shifted trying to sleep but god-damnit I have a habit of burying my face in his neck while sleeping hugging him tightly.. his cologne was all over me and I loved it

I check the time it was 2 in the morningMaybe he is sleeping peacefully that I amNot there? Or maybe he is out there drinking?

I sat up leaning my head back on the headboardI couldn't do this thats it..

I walk out of this bedroom and heading towards our bedroom I stood there staring at the door for good 5 minutes

Then I bit my lip and slowly opened the door, the room was filled with darkness so I couldn't see anything I slowly stepped inside the room closing it and locking it

I blinked a few times then I saw harry laying on the bed on his side facing the wall

Yeah...he is having his great sleep without meI walk towards the bed and laid down putting my phone on nightstand I faced harry his muscle-y back on me I laid really far from him and there was a sudden urge to be close to him

I move a little closer, a little more, a little little more and his heat now brushed my skin but I still wasn't hugging him

Before I could stop myself my fingers went up and touched his bare back and I froze hisshoulders were tensed...that means he is, I gulped.. awake

"Harry" I whisper

He moves a little and my fingers fall from his back "not now alexa" he muttered

"look.. I-I was scared because I-" he cut meOff

"I don't wanna fucking know" he growled

I flinched, blinking at his back not knowing what to say

He sat up and I couldn't see his face but I could see his dark eyes they were on my face burning holes "I fucking don't know what to do, you always fuck my mind and I." He stopped clenching his jaw "I should be mad at you which I am for you called that son of a bitch at home without me knowing? What would fucking happened if i haven't arrived at right time?" He asked me gritting his teeth "Answer me Alexa I am asking a fucking question" he warned me

I shook my head as I try my hardest to push back the tears "I-I don't know" I say quietly

"He would've done anything! Any.fucking.thing.. to you! To the person who I fucking love more than anything and what could I do? huh? Fucking nothing" he raised his voice

I flinched getting scared of him "I- I am sorry" i mumble

he sighed running his hands in his thick hair "come here" he say, I fiddle with my fingers and slowly move towards him

He picked me up like I weigh nothing and put me down on his lap so I was straddling him

I still didn't meet his gaze his rough hands come to my cheek caressing it "look at me" he says softly

I look up at him and my lower lip tremble and tears finally fall down my eyes and he froze his eyes widened "fuck!" He say he wipe my tears quickly and bring me close to him hugging me tightly my face burying in his neck, a soft sob escaped my lips

"Hey..hey.. shit Fuck! i am so.. so sorry baby" he mumbled softly to me as his hands went up and down my back his face nuzzled in my hair "I am so fucking sorry baby.. I... oh my god... Fuck I am an idiot" he said

My body shake a little as i cry silently

"Baby I am so sorry I am really fucking sorry I shouldn't have said that to you I was really scared I could lose you.." he say holding me tight against him

I looked up at him and he wiped my tears kissing my forehead his eyes were filled with nothing but guilt

I shake my head lightly as he frown a little, confused

"It-it wasn't your fault, I-I am sorry I didn't to-told you I know you're scared to lose me I am sorry I am so stup-" he put a finger on my lips softly

"No" he says simply

I smile weakly at him, he smiled back pressing his forehead with mine "fuck I made you cry" he whispered

"No, I cried because I felt how you must've felt if I ever left you.." i cupped his cheek "just like how would i react if you would've.." I stopped not wanting to complete the sentence

"I would never" he say simply then leaning in and kissing me softly not rushing just softly like I was the most delicate thing in the world

After our soft makeout sesh, I still laid on top of him cause I loved it his hands wrapped around my waist pulling me so close to him a blanket drape over us I lay my head in his neck nuzzling my face in it loving the warmth and his cologne my favourite cologne I kissed his neck softly again and again and i heard a low growl escape from his throat"Don't do that or I'll fuck you so bad you would be sore for a whole week" he whispered in my ear seductively, his deep voice filled with hunger

Oh god

Not nowSorry I need a good sleep now monkey face

My face grow all red and i nuzzled my face in his neck hiding in deeper he chuckled smacking my ass playfully he kissed my head "sleep"

And then i drift off to sleep just how I like itHim

...

Part 28

A lexa

Harry took a leave today because he said he wanted to spend more time with me I planned a whole day that we'll be cuddling and watching movies

A notification appeared on my phone I opened it

'Alexa, its me' Unknown number

I frown looking at the msg What the hell do you mean by its me?

'I am sorry but I don't seem to know who 'me' is' I reply putting my phone down

I tried to grab the suitcase thats over the cupboard but I couldn't grab it as I am really short and so now I need harryHis ass must be watching cricket he is a real big fan of it so he's always watching matches

"Harry" i call him

He doesn't answer

"Harry!!" I say more louder

Silence

Is he grown deaf?

"Giant Big foot handsome man with chimpanzee's face bring your ass up here!" I yell

No response, No zilch nada

I pick my phone and msg him

'Harry come up here before I murder u with my own bare hands u stupid ass face'

My phone dinged and he replied"

Seriously?

Then I heard a door twist and he came in with a bored expression

"Why weren't you answering me?" I say folding my arms

"I didn't heard you" he shrug

I narrow my eyes "dont you dare lie to me"

"Baby, why would I lie to you" he said it like it would be a crime.. and yes it would be

And then it hit me"Oh, this room must be soundproof" I nod in under-standing

I turn to look at harry and he had a tiny smirk with devilish expression playing on his face

Okay he is ready to do some sin

He came towards me wrapping his arm around my waist

He lean down to whisper "then why don't we take advantage of that and I'll make you scream my name" he lean back with smirk still playing and his one eyebrow raised

I blush red at his words hitting his arm playfully

His smirk grew wider

"I swear to god harry shutup" I say still blushing

"Okay wifey" he winks at me before pecking my lips softly

"I need your little hand by bringing that suitcase down I can't reach it" i say sighing

He look at his hands "little" he repeats the word with a tiny amused expression in his eyes

"Oh shit sorry I mean your biggest hand in the world even bigger than big foot's hand. Okay? Sounds better?" I ask him with serious expression trying to control my laugh

He glares at me with unamused expression

And then a laugh escaped my mouth I laughed my ass off looking at harry who wanted to kill me that time I cough "okay okay i'll stop" I say breathing in and out

His hand reached up and he brought the suitcase down "there you go"

"thankyou thankyou thankyou I love you" I say cooing and he smiles in return

Ah I would die for that smile

-

We are in theatre room all cuddled up with a blanket wrapped around us

"No we are not watching that" he made a disgusting face when I clicked 'Beauty and the Beast'

"Oh come on its a great movie" I gave him a look

He rolled his eyes "no"

I pout "pleasee" doing puppy eyes

His eyes went down on my lips then leaning down and capturing it in a soft kiss He nuzzle his nose with mine "nope" he whisper popping the 'p'

I drop the remote sighing with anger my nose flared as I lean back from cuddling him he frowns at me, I remove the blanket from me then folding my arms "okay, you choose the movie" I say to him more like challenge him

he sigh "okay"

"Okay, choose" I say gesturing towards the movie

"No I am saying okay we can....watch 'Beauty and the Beast'.. now come here" he say opening his arms

I smile widely then jump at him making him chuckle I kiss his nose then his cheeks his forehead and his lips softly he smiles softly at me "if I get this reward when I have to watch this movie, I'll watch it till the day I die"

I bit my lip smiling, I sat on his lap laying my head on his chest and my arms around his torso his large hand wrapped around my waist while one hand playing with my hairwe watch movie together

"Look harry" I say pointing at the screen

I look back at him and froze he was soundly sleeping breathing softly, I smile at him resting my chin on his chest watching his pretty face I tilt my head lightly, he's just so precious to me I don't know how did I found the perfect person, I would choose him over anyone

I kiss his lips softly for 2 seconds I lean back and he stir in his sleep

I don't wanna wake him up but I really want him to sleep upstairs otherwise his body would pain

I shake him lightly "harry" i whisper softly at him, he looks so peaceful and angel while sleeping his locks falling on his forehead making him look more cute

I bring my hand up to cup his cold cheeks he stir a little moving closer to my hand, wanting more warmth

"Baby, we need to sleep but not here, upstairs" I slowly hug him nuzzling my face in his neck and his mouth-watering cologne filled my nose

"okay" he mumble in his low deep gruff voice

I swear to god i love his sleepy voice That makes me so turned on

After a few seconds I try to get up but he tighten his hold on me and gets up I was still in his arms straddling him like a baby, i didn't argued as i loved being like this

He walked us towards the elevator and we get inside it his hand were under my thigh holding me tight against him he burried his face in my hair sighing

he lead us to our room and closed it locking it, walking towards our bed he dropped us both and i landed on top of him

He groans slowly "I love this position" he mutters as i lay on top of him straddling him

He hugged me even tighter then kissing my head "sleep, love" he whispers and i smile at him even tho he couldn't see my face

After a few minutes i heard his soft calm breaths and i knew he has slept my phone dinged with notification and i somehow struggled and picked my phone

'Your mother' Unknown Number

My phone slipped of my hand as it drop on bed making my eyes widen with shock

how?.. i-it couldn't- no no, it can't be

It was the same number that messaged me

What do she need now?

......

VOTE COMMENT

LOVE Y'ALL

Part 29

Harry

The deal that my dad told me is still going in my head its messing with my mind

I didn't said yes to the deal But he still asked me to think about it

What about Alexa?

A thought crosses my mind How would she react?

I could never talk about this with alexa cause this is the weirdest shitty deal but somehow it still benefits me

'You have to sleep one night with me harry and your dad will not ask for any money nor will he bother you'My fucking step - mother's words went through my mind again

I could never cheat alexa, never in my wildest dreams

i was too shock to speak when my dad also agreed to her conditionBut how does it benefit him? I am fucking sure he is playing some mind games with me

"Sir" ana's voice brought me back from my thoughts

I clear my throat "yes, Ana"

"Your coffee" she places the coffee on the table with a smile

I nodded "Thankyou I would be going home now" I tell her picking my phone up and standing up

"Yes sir" she nodded

"You can also go home if you're done"

"Ofcourse sir, Have a great day" she smiles

My lip twitch a little "you too"

I make my way outside sitting in my car and driving back home Today I drove myself here

I saw a flower shop at my right side I thought of buying it for Alexa she loves flowers

I parked the car getting out of the car i shut the door buttoning up my suit jacket I walked inside the shop

There was the old man sitting over there "how may I help you son?" He asked soft smile on his face

I smiled at him "sir I would like a bouquet of roses for my wife"

He grins nodding he gets up picking the nice heavy bouquet he gave it to me

"Thankyou, how much sir?" I asked him taking my wallet out

"3 dollars" he say smiling "one of my grand-daughter is getting married this week so I am selling these flowers to save"

My heart filled with warmth as he said that I smiled at him

I took the 1000 dollar and gave it to him

"Oh son I don't have the change"

I smile at him and shook my head "its for you sir if you need more I can gi-" he cuts me off

"No no! Thankyou so much that is really kind of you but I can't take that much money" he had wrinkles on his eyes as he blink

"Its nothing.. keep it please" I gave it to him

"Thankyou so much son!" He hugged me I froze but hugged him back

He back off with a grin

Will 1000 be enough for his grand-daughter's marriage?

No of course not

I took one of my credit card out "Sir, this is the gift from me to you for helping your grand-daughter's marriage that is really lovely" I gave the credit card to him telling him the pin "it has 10,000 dollars in it"

He stood there frozen one of the tear trickle down his eyes "y- who are you? My own son didn't even helped me a-and you... you are Amazing... I- I don't have any words" his voice breaks

I shake my head smiling a little "i am nobody...thankyou for flowers sir i'll be going"

"Thankyou again!!" He say loudly

I smile nodding

I sit back in my car droving off

I parked my car, entering inside the house I held the bouquet behind me

"Lex?" I call

no reply

"Sweetheart where are you?" I call once again louder this time

She must be in the room, I took the stairs rushing upstairs going to my bedroomI slowly opened it and watched the lights were dim, tv was on and there she was on the bed laying down curled in a ball wearing

My hoodie

A sudden wave of warmth hit me as a smile appeared on my face

She didn't noticed me as she was busy watching the tv

I close the door and she turned towards me and then she smiled "harry" her voice small

I frown, I walk up to her sitting beside her she was still laying curled in a ball I tug one of her strands behind her hair pecking her lips softly "What happened my baby?" I ask in a soft tone

She pouted "periods"

"Oh that damn fucker" I sayShe chuckled slowly, I smile at her

Alexa have the worst period cramps she can't sit properly because of the pain, I suggested that we could go to the doctor but she is afraid of the doctors so everytime I ask her she says no

She looked sad I cupped her cheeks pressing my forehead with hers "Whats wrong?" I whisper

"I planned that we could watch a movie together then have a lot of sex"

I chuckled shaking my head "another time"

"Yeah whatever another time" she roll her eyes

Okayyyy mood swings

"Okay wait here i'll be right back" I tell her she just nods

I hid the flowers under the bed before walking out I quickly rushed towards my car getting in it I went to nearby supermarket

I grabbed candies, chocolates, sweets following with some crackers, bags of Doritos, Pringles

I quickly bought all of them and went home

Then I took all of the snacks to our room and she was still laying

I gave her all the snacks and her face light up like its christmas she grinned like a fucking cute babyI clear my throat hiding my smile I gave the flowers to her "for you" I say smiling

she looked at the flowers, snacks and then at me with a 'aww' face I saw her eyes shine and her lower lip tremble

Fuckk

"D-do you not like these flowers? Or snacks?"I ask with guilt on my face

She shook her head and started crying

Fuck you totally messed up

I quickly brought her in my lap and hugged her she twisted my shirt in her fist burrying her face in my chest she sobbed I rubbed her back soothing her, I kissed her head "I am sorry, I-" she cuts me off

"N-no they are the best! I love them" she sob

Then why is she-

Ah mood swings

I hugged her tight against me soothing her "its okay baby" I whisper in her hair running my hand in her hair

After she cried for 15 minutes she finally backed off with puffy eyes I wipe her tears and she smiled at me

I cup her cheeks and she leans in closing her eyes "I don't like you crying" I say

She sniffed "I cried because I was overwhelmed"

"oh really? Are you sure" I tease her

She opened her eyes I smiled then She glared at me and my smile dropped

Okay- this ain't working

I clear my throat "w-whats for dinner?" I changed the topicBecause I am damn scared of Alexa when she is on her periods that woman could kill you

"I didn't cook because I was having cramps" she pouted

I cupped her chin bringing her close to me I kissed her nose then pecking her lips "hey... its alright I can order takeaway"

She smiled then cuddled with me burrying her face in my neck inhaling "you always smell so damn good" she say "I love you" she smiles in my neck

I kissed the top of her head interlocking my fingers with her I caress her knuckles with my thumb "I love you more"

....

Hellooo My People!Soo I've been really busy! But I still write as much as I can

Big chapters are coming up! Buckle up!!

LOVE Y'ALL

Part 30

AuthorTHANKYOUUU SO MUCH GUYS FOR SHOWERING YOUR LOVE BY READING MY STORY! I WISH I COULD HUG Y'ALL KEEP SHOWERING YOUR LOVE!!!

This is a Big ass chapter so buckle up! ;) for twists and shocks

Alexa

"Harry" I say twirling spaghetti in my fork not eating it

"yes" he sips his juice looking at me

I clear my throat "you know about the job I...haven't talked to you about it and you know how much I love working so.." I stop biting my lip, he raises an eyebrow

"Can I work at Jack's again?" I ask biting inside of my cheek turning my head

He puts his fork down turning himself to me "Baby.. working at jack's is the last thing i'll ask you to do" I sigh averting my eyes from him, he continues "but... if you like to work that much I can help you find some suitable jobs"

My head snap to him "really?" I ask trying my best to hide the excitement

"Yes.. if that's what you like" he shrugs

"Oh I would love it" I say grinning he chuckle in his breath

.As Harry promised he found me some jobs and he had asked me to decide which one will be more comfortable to me

And all of them had good pays

"Yeah this one" I say to harry

He took the laptop and focuses narrowing his eyes his jawline sharp ready to cut a diamond and I am so grateful to have this hot ass person as my husband I thank god everyday!

When I wake up It takes me an hour to process thoughts:- is this hot nugget laying beside me really my husband? - Like are you sure you married him?- There is no in the hell way you got this lucky - Why is he so eatable?

He hums and I shook my thoughts away "this one is alright" he nods "okay you can start it from tomorrow"

"Great" I say clapping my hand he passes me a small smile

It was as a barista in one of the big cafes Thankfully harry agreed to what I wanna work as, he supports me and I can't be more thankful

His phone rings and he picks up the smile on his face vanished he furrow his eyebrows "I am sorry who?" He asks confused

He shook his head then looks at me "Alexa?" He repeats the name as in confirming

"What?" I mouthed, he showed me his index finger as a 1 minute

"No she does not I am sorry this is wrong num-" he stops then sigh "no I am afraid I can't let you talk to her"

"Harry who is it? Give me the phone" I say

"I am sorry Ma'am this is the wrong number" he says again sternly, ignoring me

I leaned forward and took his phone "Alexa" he tries to grab the phone

"Harry a minute" I gave him the look

He sigh nodding

I took the phone "Hello who is it?" I ask

I heard the person on phone take the sharp intake of breath "A-alexa...honey" she said slowly

It took me a moment to realise but when I did my eyes went wide as the phone dropped from my hand

My hand started to shiver hearing that voice my mouth agape as I stare the wall shockingly

I felt harry shake me but I couldn't process I could only hear my heart pounding faster in my chest he cupped my cheek and forced me to look at him his face was pale and his eyes were wide with fear clearly visible in his eyes

I blink and felt my eyelids getting heavy "h-harry" my voice small and croaked

Then I blacked out and felt everything go black

.

"I DON'T FUCKING KNOW!" I heard a loud deep familiar voice yelling

I couldn't see the face as my eyes were closed

"YOU FUCKING WAKE HER UP!" The voice come again

"S-sir we are trying" another voice I can't seem to recognise came

"FUCK OFF ALL OF YOU" the familiar voice yells again

I release a slow breathe slowly opening my eyes

"Alexa" a heard that voice soften

I blink and closed my eyes tightly due to the light

"CLOSE THE FUCKING LIGHTS!" He order someone and I heard the light switched off

I opened it again blinking, I gulp looking around I was in our room and there was a staff of hospital standing at the corner of the room I turn around and saw harry his face showed worry, fear he was wearing grey sweatpants and black shirt his hair was a mess looking like he ran his fingers through it alot of time

He took steps towards me and sat beside me holding my hand with shivering hands I frown at him he release a shaky breathe pressing his forehead with mine "baby" he whispers

I was trying to figure out what's the problem because I could sense something isn't right

I cup harry's cheeks caressing it I look at the staff "C-can you give us a moment?" I say my voice hoarse

Harry look over them probably glaring at them they quickly nodded and left

When they left closing the door harry dropped his face on my chest burying it he release another shaky breathe

I hugged him tightly close to me, confused

"Hey...what's wrong please tell me" I whisper softly

"Y-you were not waking up...." He says taking another deep breathe I had many questions but I listened to him I ran my fingers through his hair silently telling him to continue "for a week..I- I was so scared" his voice broke

I bit my lip trying my best not to cry I closed my eyes "I am sorry.. I am so.. so sorry" I whisper

He looks up and his eyes were wet that made my hug him once again "don't cry please don't.... i am sorry I am sorry" my lower lip started to tremble

We stayed in each other's embrace for a long time I was confused that I was blacked out for a whole week..

.

"And you just need to take these medicines, You'll be Fine" the doctor says handling his prescription to Harry he nodded

I nodded "thankyou doctor" I say softly

He smiled and looked at harry "I'll be going now"

Harry nodded and thanked him aswell shaking his hand

He took the doctor and I looked at ceiling

What happened before I had blacked out

Yeah.. my mother called harry why did she?

Harry came back sitting on the armchair beside our bed he looked at me carefully "how are you feeling?" He ask

"Good" I bit my inside cheek "harry why did.." i clear my throat "the woman that called you did you find out who was she?"

He furrow his eyebrows looking at the wall "she said you are her daughter and I don't know why would some-" I cut him off

"She was right" I say hurriedly

He frowns deeply looking at me he opens his mouth and closed not knowing what to say

"She....she was my mother and that's why I faint hearing her voice after a long.. long time"

"Alexa is this a joke?" He asks again his jaw clenched

I knew he was angry he had every right to be, but right now I was just confused how did she got harry's number

"Alexa" he says again sternly

I shake my thoughts away "this is not a joke, I.." I stopped not knowing how to explain him

He gets up pushing the chair away I flinch at the harshness "Do you know How much I was fucking scared that who that woman was or what she could've said to you" his nose was flared and his eyes showed rage "what she could've said that made you fucking faint.." his voice grew louder his jaw clenched and his lips in thin line

"I- I am sorry I was gonna tell you but when I heard her voice the flashbacks of her sweet voice filled me and I.. I fainted" I bit my lip hesitantly staring at harry

He looked away not making eye contact he closed his eyes taking deep breathes calming himself down

He opened the drawer taking the packet of cigarette out with lighter

Wha-?

He sat down again looking at me he took one of the cigarette out and put it in his mouth lighting it he inhaled it releasing the smoke

I scrunch my eyebrows but didn't said anything I knew when he was stressed or worried he smoke so I never stopped him

"What did she say" he asks quietly

"She just said Alexa honey thats it"

He clicks his tongue rubbing his thumb on his eyebrow closing his eye "I am gonna find out how did she get my number" he tells

I nod "okay" I reply

We stayed quiet for a long time staying in silence

He gets up throwing his cigarette in dustbin "I am going out I'll be late don't wait for me" he says without making eye contact

"Okay..be.." I say but he closed the door walking out "safe.." I finished sighing

I cleaned up changing into my sweats I walk down the stairs going into kitchen I tied my hair in a bun and started cooking Spaghetti with meat-balls

It was harry's favourite

I finally cooked it smiling Now we wait for harry

I walk to lounge area and sat there opening the tv on I clicked netflix and started watching 'never have I ever'

From one episode to two whole seasons I watched it and harry was still not home

My eyelids starting getting heavy and I slept

.

I heard a loud door bang open I quickly sat up rubbing my eye I look around and saw harry coming inside his white shirt was not as crisp as he wears his sleeves were rolled up and his hair was a mess

He started walking and then I realise he was drunk

Oh dear lord help me

I quickly walk up to him and he stepped back dropping a vase it broke I gasp and he look back "oopsie" he say putting his finger on his lips

I quickly sat down collecting the pieces He sat down as well "stop it you're gonna hurt yourself" he says quietly

I didn't heard him and collected the pieces I threw it away and I came back to harry

"Why are you drunk?" I ask

He chuckles sending warm feeling in my chest "I am not drunk baby" he says chuckling again

Oh he was definitely drunk

"Harry come on lets go up" I say putting his arm around my shoulder

I groan Damnn this gorilla was heavy

I took him up to the room and he dropped himself on the bed chuckling again I shake my head and remove his shoes socks

I heard his soft snores and I knew he slept I slowly climbed up on the bed drifting of to sleep

Harry

I woke up groaning my head was aching alot

Shit

I look at my side and saw alexa sleeping looking like an angel she looked so pretty I moved on of the strand of her hair that was annoying her she moved closer to me and I felt my features softened a soft smile on my face

I slowly get up not to wake her up I went to bathroom showering freshening up I took the pill for headache and drink the water gulping the pill down my throat

I sigh and kept the glass aside I look over to Alexa and she was still sleeping

Yeah I was angry yesterday because I care alot and I could never think of losing Alexa

I walk up to her softly kissing her forehead and leaving

My phone rang and I pick it up "Hello" I say

"Meet me at the Danz' cafe at 8pm" I heard a women's voice say

I frown "Who are you?"

"I'll tell you its urgent just meet me there" she says

There must be any danger but I plan on taking security with me I sigh "Okay"

.

After I was done with work I checked my watch and it was 7:50

I took security with me but they were dressed in casuals so she wouldn't find out

They all had guns even me I made my way inside danz' cafe and look around

A manager approached me "Mr. Stewart" he smiled I nod

"Sir there is a lady who has booked a seat for you two should I take you to her?" He ask politely

"Yes, thankyou" I say he nods and guides me towards the elevator

We went to second floor and there was a lady sitting there and I couldn't see her face as she had her back on me

"This is it sir, I'll send the waiters" he says

I nod and he left

I clear my throat and she turned towards me

I froze blinking

Flashbacks came in my mind

"Mom! Mom!" I call as I ran inside the house

Today I got an A+ in my maths test that I have been working hard for

I saw mom in the kitchen "harry!" She smiled at me

I loved her smile

"Mom look I got an A+" I showed her the report card she looked at it and grinned

She hugged me "you are such an intelligent boy..my boy" she say

She backed off from hug "you know I love you right?" Her eyes were shining

I didn't know why was she crying I nodded and asked "Mom. Don't you like that I got an A+?"

She wiped her tears sniffing "no baby Mom is not crying you just made her so happy" she send me a weak smile

"Mom you promise?" I ask

She smiles and nods "Yes I promise"

I smile and wipe her tears "okay mom but please don't cry I don't like you crying"

That made her cry more and she hugged me tightly

"H-harry?" Her voice brought me back

I release a shaky breathe backing off shaking my head "this can't be" I whisper to myself

How come I didn't recognised her voice when she called

She gets up and her eyes started to shine "Harry you're a big boy now" she sends me a weak smile

I frown "Who.Are.You?" I ask

She blinks "I..I am your mother" she says

"No...no no No! She died goddamnit!" I raise my voice

"I did not died that day...there is something that you don't know harry...and you need to know" she says interlocking his fingers looking at me with hope

Like hell I'll listen to her

"No.. don't you dare come near me or contact me again, my mother fucking died" I point my finger at her "Stay away" I whisper but she heard

She tried taking a step but I yell "STOP" she flinches at my tone and stopped

I rushed and walked away

The manager came towards me "sir, is that woman bothering you? Or is there-" I cut him off

"No its nothing, she's not bothering me" she is

I quickly say and walk out getting in my car I sped through the streets my knuckles were white from the hard grip

Another flashback came

"BECAUSE OF YOU! MY SOFIA DIED!" Father yelled at me again that night

"N-no dad" I say quietly

He took his belt out and beat me with it for many hours

He dropped the belt and I didn't even whimper because if I used to cry more he used to beat me more

My stepmother came inside the room "come on leave him" she say to dad throwing me a disgusting glare

Father came up to me and slapped me hard across the face and left closing the door

A sob escaped my mouth and I started to cry my heart out staring up the sky "mom.. why did you left? Do you think its my fault? I am sorry Mom I could've come with you" I say and cry more

I gasp and flashback ended a tear escaped and I wipe it

I park the car and rushed upstairs

Alexa was sitting on the bed using her phone she looked at me and smiled but then her smile disappeared as she took in my whole presence

"H-harry"she says quietly

Alexa

He told me everything that happened and I felt that everything stopped

Her birth mom was alive!

He stood up aggressively and his nose flared he walked up to the wall and he punched it again and again his knuckles started to bleed my eyes wide in horror and I quickly rushed towards him

"No!" I yelled at harry trying to stop him "harry! Stop!" I tried to stop him

But he kept on doing that he stepped away grabbing his hair tightly and screaming loudly

My heart shattered seeing him like that

I kept my arm around his neck trying to stop him His chest rise and fall with anger breathing heavily

"Please... please don't hurt yourself" i mumble softly

I look up at him and saw he was shaking with anger his eyes were bloodshot red

I hugged him tightly wrapping my arm around his neck caressing his back "Please calm down please" i whisper to him

He stood straight not hugging me nor doing anything he just stood there

Then after some time he broke and hugged me back tightly burrying his face in my neck "I am done" he whispered

"I am fucking done with everyone" he whispered

I run a hand in his hair "i understand" i said quietly "I am really really sorry.." I say tears prickle down my eyes as I calm him down

He dropped down to his knees hugging me from my stomach crying "I can't do this anymore lex... I can't" his voice broke as he hugged me tightly burying his face in my stomach

I run my finger through his hair pressing his head to my stomach "It's okay.. everything's gonna be okay.. I am here" I whisper

I drop down to my knees as well and he looked at me with teary eyes "tell me why does it keep happening to me... Am I that worst?" He whisper

I cup his cheeks wiping his tears away i took a breathe "no.. no you are the best.. you are amazing I can't even thank god enough that I have you.." I say pressing my forehead with his he closes his eyes

"Please don't cry... I am here..Please" I say softly

He shake his head "I can't hold it in... let me cry"

I hugged him tightly and he buried his face in my neck sobbingHis chest shake lightly as he cry

I caress his back trying to calm him down whispering sweet things to him

That night I saw harry that was completely broken, harry who couldn't face the world, the weak harry... but the fact I love him even more now this made me love him even more

That how he handles himself or how he controls himself.. but today he broke

I couldn't see tears in his grey eyes those beautiful eyes were red and those smily lips were trembling.. nothing..I say nothing broke me ever than that day seeing him like this He is my whole world my light my happiness because of him I am alive..

'He is more myself than I am, and Whatever our souls are made of.. his and mine are the same.."   Emily Brontë

....

This chapter was emotions of rollercoasterI got so emotional writing when harry broke..This proves that no one is perfect and no one is that much strong But I still will say that harry is really strong! even alexa! Both of them! Please do comment how did you like the chapter

More big chapters will come!

I love Y'all!

Part 31

<hr>

Mature Content   Alexa

Harry has been really sad and down nowadays I find ways to keep him smiling keep him happy but the smile on his face stays for a heartbeat

He been having flashbacks and nightmares thats why I always hug him close to me when he is sleeping Now you may be wondering when he sleeps I must also sleep that time but no, he works whole night and when he comes home I hold him close to me and he sleeps for only some hours Dark circles are visible under his eyes

Today I will take him to doctor because he really need to come back in his normal routine

As in for my mother she didn't contacted me after that, Harry researched on her and he find out that she is here in this city and it scares me because I don't want to see her face

"Yes logan he have been going through all this.." I say sighing

"Oh my god he did not told me!" He says on the phone

"It is not his fault logan, my poor baby is going through all this how is he suppose to tell you all this please try to understand and come at my house we have to take him to the hospital" I check the time

"Okay... I'll be there in 15 minutes" He say

"Okay be there soon, bye" I hung up, walking upstairs

Harry is sleeping and its 3 in the afternoon I got in our room seeing harry who was sleeping

He flinches in his sleep "no.. no no Mom!" He mutters, his face pained as he moves

"i-I am sorry dad!" He says louder still stirring in his sleep I quickly rush over him and grab his hand

"Hey... baby I am here.. I am here its okay" I whisper caressing his cheek kissing his forehead

He stops stirring and opens his eyes slowly He saw me sitting beside and his lazy gaze on me his features softened and a hint of smile passed his lips

"You need to freshen up... we need to go to doctor" I say

He frowns and sits up he cups my cheek "what happened to you? are you feeling okay? Is it fever? What's wrong-" I cut him off

"No stop, it is not about me" I take his hand that was cupping my cheek to his cheek and he cupped his cheek frowning at me "it is about you.."

"No I am not going to doctor" He looks at me like I've grown mad

"Yes you are" I state

"No" he folds his arms

"Yes" I say sternly

"No" He says more sternly

Well you asked for it

I made best puppy eyes blinking at him "pleasee" I pout

He groans "this is cheating"

I smirk internally, He grabs my face and pressed his soft lips to mine He softly move his lips around mine like if he leaves me I'll vanish we kiss for sometime and he backs off licking his lips "I missed this" He whisper his voice more deep

I bit my lip "me too but" he frowns "we'll continue it when we come back right now logan is coming" I pursue my lips

He stays stunned "That motherfucker?"

A giggle escapes my lips "yes but no" i frown "don't use cuss words"

He rolls his eyes "He is a mother-" I press my palm to his mouth and he mumbles on my palm his nose scrunches

Aww cute

He stops mumbling and kiss my palm I smile at him and shake my head

The doorbell rang and I asked him to freshen up

I open the door and saw logan standing with a massive, yea massive smile on his face following with a bouquet

"Hi logan" I smile

"Heyy sister in law" he winks

I stare at him boringly while he had a goofy grin, I move aside "Come in"

He grins and comes inside

"Harry is upstairs freshening up when he'll come downstairs we'll go" I tell him and he nods

We sat in lounge chatting about somethings and logan told me that he just found a girl who he thinks is perfect for him her name is stella and he have started having feelings for her and Im so damn happy for him he really deserves a girl

"Now look" he says I turn towards him and raise an eyebrow

"You need to make her jealous" he pursue his lips

I frown "what?"

"Listen to me first okay?" He says I nod "okay, so Stella's friend told me that she is a jealous kinda girl like a bad girl and I like that you know like wild cat the one who could bite yo-" I cut him off

"Logan please skip the part" I say blinking at him

He chuckles awkwardly "yeah... sure, so as I was saying you need to comment on my picture on Instagram any comment that would make her jealous because her friend said that she only feels jealous when someone is close to her or something like that.. so you down?" He asks with hopeful eyes

"Uh...ye-" a voice cut me off

"Never"

I turn around and saw harry standing behind us wearing black t shirt with black jeans his hands in his pockets and his hair slightly wet from shower his jawline sharp as ever his grey eyes narrowed on logan ready to kill him

He takes steps towards us and his addictive cologne filled me I closed my eyes for a second enjoying it I opened my eyes and saw him looking at me with a tiny smirk on his face I blush and glared him his smirk widened

Logan cleared his throat, and we both turned towards him "Alexa please" he says

"Logan.. yeah sure I'd help you" I say nicely

Harry sit beside me looking at me with disbelief "There in no fucking way you're helping him"

I pursue my lips "Please?"

He blinks at me "No"

"Harry come on" Logan says

Harry glares at him "You shut the fuck up before I kick you out of here"

"Ha-" logan tries to say but harry showed him his middle finger but harry's gaze on me

Harry leans down to my ear "Convince me" he whispers

I try my best not to shiver infront of logan This is soo awkward

I turn towards logan "Uh logan? Give us a moment please?"

He nods "suree" he walks upstairs

I turn towards harry "Then don't complain"

"Oh I would never" a sexy smirk on his lips

I was wearing a skirt that reached my upper thigh following with black stockings and a red top

I straddle his lap and he looks at me with amazement

I lean forward and my breast pressed against his hard chest I kiss his lips teasing his bottom lip with my tongue He opens his mouth gladly and I slide my tongue inside his mouth dominating him I kissed him hungrily I started grinding myself on his hard dick he groans and grab my hips harshly

I lean back and a grin spread on his lips he rub his thumb on his bottom lip "you are a dirty little vixen... my vixen" he whispers looking down at my lips then up in my eyes

My hand went down to his growing erection I squeeze it through his pants and he groan lowly throwing his head back I undo his pants and he removes it halfway I remove his boxers and I saw his hard rock manhood free out of his boxers

"Baby.." he cups my cheek whispering "its risky doing this but...you'll look to sexy getting caught" he tilt his head licking his lips "too fucking sexy" he says lowly

I smirk and touch his lips "well maybe I like the idea of getting caught with you" he looks at me with shocked and amusement then

He claims my mouth hungrily kissing me my hand went around to grab his dick I move my hand up and down and he groans in my lips "you'll be the death of me" he mutters in my mouth and I smile I look up and saw logan was nowhere "what if he hears us?" I ask He bit his lip "let him listenmy name"

His hands went up to cup my already wet sex, he looks me in the eye his mouth opened a little as he looks at me hungrily "always looking so fucking gorgeous" He remove my underwear to my knees and spank my ass putting my skirt down "ride my cock like you can't live without it" He lean back rubbing his thumb on his bottom lip staring at me with those half lids lustful eyesI put my hand on his muscular arms and he take small breaths

I slide down my eyes roll down shutting my mouth not to cry out in pleasure his hands grab my ass tightly moving me back and forth I moan lightly and bit my lip I hide my face in his shoulder biting there not to moan he moves us up and down and I heard his harsh breaths near my ear His sweet mouth found my neck sucking there I gasp near his ear nibbling it he threw his head back

We finish up as fast as we could I stare at him panting his hair stick to his forehead as his head leaned back his eyes closed I got out from his lap and I hiss his hands found my inner thigh and he run his hand up and down there massaging it lightly he kiss my inner thigh and got up putting his pants up buttoning it

"Thankgod Logan didn't came down" I sigh

"He must be asleep" He shrugs

"Don't just shrug go and check on him" I say folding my arms

He shake his head a smirk on his face "so bossy"

"Just for you" I wink

Amusement playing in his eyes "it should be" He went up to get logan while I went in washroom fixing myself, I went to kitchen to grab some juice

I heard harry's voice "He really was sleeping"

I chuckle shaking my head "is he awoke?"

"Yeah fuckface is washing his face" I hear his footsteps coming down

"Harry" I say in warning voice

"Baby" he says in same tone

I bit back a smile, I felt his strong arms wrap around my torso "why do you always smell so good?" I ask

I felt him smile on my neck he placed a soft kiss there

"Come on love birds we not to go" logan said

I turn around facing logan "yeah sure"

"And do you talked to harry about helping me?" He asked

I felt heat crawl up to my neck I nod "mhm"

Harry was grinning like an idiot

God this guy

......

Part 32

This chapter is dedicated to my lovely reader 'aannaannyyaa10' Thankyou so much for supporting me! I love you with all my heart□□ Keep reading!□

Alexa

"And you need to come back to your normal routine harry, you hear me?" I ask sternly

He stares at the traffic infront of him boringly then nodding "yes"

"And you better take the medicines that doctor gave you"

He nods mumbling "yes" running his fingers through his hair then putting it back on steering wheel

We went to doctor and there isn't anything to worry about he will be fine and his routine will get better

Harry is driving while I am in the passenger seat and logan on the backseat staring at his phone since we got inside the car

I commented on his picture 'Handsome' with thousands of emojis

Harry doesn't know what I commented and maybe thats why he is so calm while logan is waiting for stella to do something

"You hungry?" Harry asked looking at me for a moment then back at the front

"I want to go to McDonalds" I mumble pouting

He took my hand that was resting on my lapand kissed it "yes my love" now holding my hand

We went through drive thru and then went home I asked him if we could eat at home because I was in no mood to eat here

We sat on dining table and I took my nuggets grinning

Three things I love in life

HarryDonutsNuggets

Harry wasn't hungry and so wasn't logan so it was just me

We dropped logan home and came here

I eat my nuggets and looked at harry who was looking at me with a soft smile on his face, he has the most precious smile

I passed my nugget to him he shook his head slowly

I shrug and eat it

"I love nuggets a lot" I said to him while eating a nugget

"And I love you" he said kissing my lips softly I smiled
And you're my nugget

Harry got a phone-call and he picked it up "What?" The softness in his voice left

He stayed silent while I chew my nugget slowly, looking at him

He stared at the ground "I said I don't fucking want to hear your voice or fucking meet you don't you understand woman?" His voice raise as he stood up in annoyance

I stood up walking towards him I run my hand up and down his arm looking in his eyes his eyes softened as he looked at me

He looked away massaging his temple "Don't Fucking call me again, you hear me?" He say in calmer voice and his face also calm showing no such emotions

He ended the call throwing the phone on the couch tugging his hair "fucking hell" he muttered

"Hey.. is everything okay?" I ask softly

He looks at me his grey eyes now a bit tired "yeah, yeah sure" he nod giving me a small smile

I sigh as I made my way towards him I took his hands rubbing my thumb on his knuckles "you know you can talk to me whenever you want right?" I mumble softly

He put his finger under my chin lifting my face up to meet his gaze "Of course sweetheart I am just a little stressed now" he cupped my cheeks "but I promise I will tell you okay?" He whisper, I nod and he kisses my forehead then hugged me sighing

he backed off from hug "I need to handle some things for now, I'll be back soon" He caresses my cheek

I nod smiling "okay"

He smile back and kisses me softly "I love you"

I smile wider "I love you too"

My phone rang and I saw it was logan

"Logan I am not commenting again" I say sighing

I heard him laugh "no no, its not that.. well Stella saw your comment and she really got jealous you know"

I chuckled "really?"

"Oh yeah, then I finally told her my plan and at first she was kinda angry but now she's fine and guess what?"

"What?"

"She is my fucking girlfriend!" He squeals

I giggle "woah logan.. Congrats"

"Its all because of you alexa you're the best!"

I grin "why thankyou, why don't you bring her someday"

"Yeah I will sure" he replies happily

I smile "great I'll talk to you then... and oh! Logan?"

"Yeah?"

"Use protection" I giggle

"Oh my Ale-" I ended the call laughing

I went up to our bedroom playing 'Moana' cuddling with pillow thinking its harry

harry calls me and i picked it up "Yes my beautiful husband"

he chuckles his chuckle sound deep and rich sending butterflies in my stomach "my gorgeous wife the door is closed, can you open it?" He asks kindly I smile

"okayy i'll be down" I ended the call

I rushed downstairs with a grin I opened the door and jumped on harry he step back with shock and a small chuckle I hugged him tightly and buried my face in his neck inhaling his scent that is my favourite

"I see someone missed me" he whispered teasingly in my ear

I look at him tilting my head "and you did not?"

"I missed you more than anything baby" He tugs a strand of my hair behind my ear, I smile and kiss his lips softly moving my lips around him he bites my lower lip gently backing off with a smirk

He walks inside closing the door "so, what were you doing?"

I was still clinging on him, I lay my head on his shoulder "oh well I got a call from logan he said stella became her girlfriend then I went up and was watching moana"

"Logan never do relationships" Harry seemed shock

"I think he likes her" I say smiling He nod "Yeah"

Harry took us both upstairs to our bedroom he gently laid me down on the bed "I'll get changed and i'll be back" he said and disappeared in bathroom

He came back wearing his boxers and his hair were wet from shower

I pat the side of my bed he gladly joined me and I cuddled with him laying my head on his chestWe watched moana together and after a hot make-out sesh we slept

"sorry" I hear a soft mumble but my eyes were closed

"I am sorry dad" It got louder

I blink and looked beside to see harry stirring in his sleep mumbling sorry again and again

I quickly cup his cheeks "shh shh my heart.. its okay" I whisper kissing his forehead

He open his eyes and looked at me lazily he closed his eyes sighing then bringing my face closer pressing his forehead with mine "Gosh, what would I do without you love?" He ask softly

I lean down and kiss his lips softly then his nose "I am here with you always"

He smile, that breathtaking smile that make my heart melt every time

He hold me close to him and slept while I ran my finger through his hair

It will be okay You're too strong babyI whisper to him and slept

.....

I love you all so much!! Thankyouu so much for reading my book□

Part 33

H arry

I don't know

These three words are just roaming in my mind, somewhere I know that she is my mother my mama but I still cannot trust her I want nothing but hug her tightly and never leave her again but I cannot something inside me is stopping me from doing so

Alexa has been really helping me through all this the nightmares are now thankfully gone as its been few months since I met mother and she hasn't contacted me since then

"I am not sure If I can wear this today" Alexa says eyeing her dress which I bought for her birthday last year and she said she loved it

Fun fact: I never saw her wearing it

"why not?" I focus my eyes on the dress

"Its just that.. it- it doesn't go with my heels" she say quickly "guess we are gonna wear it some other day" she chuckles nervously and took the dress inside the walk in closet

I followed her "but I never saw you wearing it" I push the topic

She turn around with dress on one hand she blinks "no n-no I have" she gave me a look "I have worn it, do you think I haven't!?" She says in high pitch voice

I stare at her blinking

She roll her eyes groaning "Fine!"

She puts the dress on the chair and turn towards me "So.." she clears her throat "this dress, well it is nice believe me it is. but the colour" she pursue her lips "its bad"

"You said you loved it" I say deadpanned

She looks at me annoyed "that colour looks like I just stepped out of the toilet and not a person now you know what I mean"

I make disgusting face "I am sorry I'll buy you new one and... your favourite colour" I say with guilty face

She pouts "Aww my poor baby its alright I don't need a dress, come here" she opens her arm

I smile widely like a kid would when he gets his favourite candy, she hugged me caressing my back then playing with my hair she loves to do that "you're too sweet to be true" she mumble I smile

She backs off and kisses me slowly with those soft lips she chuckled I frown her thumb went upto my lips and she wiped it "remember when I said I don't need a dress?" She asked I nod "Forget that, I need it" she said it seriously, I couldn't help but smile "your wish is my command, my queen" I took her hand and kiss it

Alexa

We are now on our way to Harry's business partner's house, its his engagement party party all of harry's partners and friends will be there so I had to dress nicely I chose the midnight blue dress which was long and went till my foot it hugged my body nicely and it was backless

Harry was fall in love all over again when he saw me wearing this dress, I like it when he compliments me I want him to do it everytime

"who's this business partner I forgot to ask" I ask harry who was caressing my knuckles with his thumb, He looked up at me "He is my great business partner, Mr John Watson, helped me through alot of things and guided me I owe him alot" He says

I smile and kissed his forehead he love it when I do it, he love all the things I do

"Who's the lady?" I asked out of curiosityHe shook his head "I don't know yet but Mr John talk about her very fondly"

"How old is he?"

"In his 50's" he replied

I nod "I think he'd be good looking just by his name you know there is a vibe that he'd be sexy man with a hot personality I bet, you know like John sexy watson" I grin

Yes he was unimpressed

Harry raises his eyebrows at me "you seem very interested in him, you should thank god your husband isn't here" he says sarcastically

I chuckle "Yes he's an ass"

"An ass you like to squeeze all the time" he shake his head

"Oh yeah, I like that booty" I lick my lips acting seductive to which his rich laugh filled the car its like music to my ears

The car came to a stop and driver opened our doors I step out and my eyes followed a large mansion infront of me which was crowded a lot

Harry snakes his arm on my waist pulling me close to him and we walk towards the entrance

We saw a guard at the entrance who looked at harry and bowed while he stared at front The door opened and It was a massive hall filled with many people not fully crowded but there was noise of people chattering laughing and some dancing on the dance floor

Harry guided us towards a man who looked in his 40, 50's Harry hugged him "Congratulations Mr John" he said smiling

"Oh how many times do I have to tell you call me John!" Mr John said loudly and chuckled his eyes then set on me "Mrs Stewart" he smiled kindly "Pleasure to meet you"

I smile back "Mr John hi, Nice to meet you"

"Harry talk about you all the time" he grins while harry smile and looks at me

I look at harry and saw love filled in his eyes I lean and kiss his lips softly to which he kisses me back

I look at Mr John "oh sorry,Congratulations on your engagement and wedding!"

He grins "Thankyou honey, Oh and I'll bring My soon to be Mrs here" he says while me and harry nodded, he disappeared in the crowd

Harry turn towards me "Would you like a drink?" I shook my head "No, but I'll wait right here you can get yours"

"Okay I'll be right back" he kisses my forehead and went towards the bar

I look around the crowd

"You must be Alexa?" A voice came from behind

I turn around and saw a lady, a gorgeous lady looking who must be in her 40's She looked stunning

I smile at her "sorry do I know you?"

She shook her head "No, I am Liana John's fiance" she smiled

"Oh! Hi! You're gorgeous" I say

"Thankyou dear" she says she look around the crowd like she was looking for someone

"Looking for Mr John?" I ask

Her head snap towards me "No I- I was looking for harry, umm John talk alot about him" she chuckles nervously

"Oh he's gone to get drink" I nod

"How's marriage life with him? Is he good? Does he take good care of you? He doesn't annoy you does he?" She ask

I smile awkwardly "Yeah.... He's...great!" I grin

A relief passes on her face she nodded and the smile plastered on her face

"Uh can I talk to you?....about somewhere private?" She says nervously biting her inside cheek

She was acting strange

I nod "sure" clearing my throat "lead the way"

She took us to balcony, I look around the view was amazing

"How long have you been married to him?" She asked

"Its been some months" I reply

"I am about to tell you something and please don't panic or don't take this wrong way listen to me at first... I really need your help" she says clasping her both hands together with hope swirling in her eyes

What is it?

I open my mouth to say No but then I closed it I sigh and tap my foot with curiosity, turning towards her I say "okay.. but make it quick"

She nods and start explaining..

Some minutes later..

My mouth agape as I stare at her "What?" My voice came out high pitched

"Yes.. harry is my son" She low her head "and I shouldn't have left him that day but... I had reasons" she look at me and a tear fall from her eyes I quickly wipe it away

"I-I am sorry for what happened and.. I really love him I can not see him like this you don't know how many nightmares he have its so heartbreaking seeing him this way.... I'll try and..." I take a deep breath "Help you"

Her eyes shine and her face stretch with big smile she hugged and thanked me

..

I look around the crowd to find Harry

Now the plan is to escape from here, Harry cannot see her today like this..
I have to explain him all this thing and have to force him to meet her and
give her a chance

I felt a hand on my shoulder I turned around

"Where were you? I was looking for you" harry said worriedly

"Oh I was in female toilet" I say smiling "and uh harry?"

He hums in response sipping his drink

"I want to go home" I blurt, his head snapped towards me he frowned
"what? Why? We just came and I-" I cut him off

"I know I know but I don't feel too good" I sigh

His face became horrified he quickly cupped my face "What happened? Is
everything alright? baby tell me" he says softly

My heart hurts lying to him so instead of acting like I am sick I'll act like I
am turned on

I stood on my tip toes and whisper in his ear "I want you...now"

I lean back and looked up at him blinking and rub my hand slowly on my
thigh his eyes followed the movement

His eyes darkened as he stared at me He exhale harshly licking his lips he
looked around He grabbed my hand "lets go" leading us outside

I smirk mentally patting myself

....

Hiii Y'all I am back!! Sorry I kmow I was gone for a long time but! I'll try and write as much as I can

Lets see what will happen in the story further ;) comment down what do you think??

Thanks for supporting <33

Part 34

Mature content Ahead(Not all of the chapter is for mature people I have mentioned down when the part has ended)

Alexa

Harry looked like he was fighting his inner demon he was tapping his foot impatiently

"George can't you drive fucking fast?" his deep voice filled with annoyance as he glared at the driver through rear mirror

"S-sir there is alot of traffic" george replied

Harry clenched his jaw and closed his eyestaking slow breaths "why the fuck did I bring the driver" he whispered to himself I bit back a smile

I watch him closely as he looked so sexy I was definitely turned on, his hair coming to his forehead his sharp jaw clenched which I want to kiss, his kissable lips in thin line as he take slow breaths from his nose, and also he smell incredibly delicious

His suit jacket was off, he lay back as his chest rose and fell, his eyes caught mine and all I could see was the darkness filled in them his strong hands went up to his tie he loosened it watching me intently It wasn't suppose to turn me on so much but it did!

I was about to jump yes jump on him when the car came to a stop

"Sir we've reached" George said, harry stepped out of the car and opened my door he took my hand and his eyes were still black with the lust

We went inside the house he closed the door and pinned me there kissing the life out of me, his lips moved desperately around mine as his one hand pinned my both hands above my head his other hand hold me tight against him

He removed his lips and we both catch our breath "you don't know what you fucking do to me" he breathe licking his lips, He leaned a little back "I will fuck you... hard, you've been a really naughty girl aren't you?" He tilted his head watching me closely, I was out of words as I stare at his gorgeous face quietly

He softly kissed my lips tugging the bottom lip and biting it gently "tell me" he mumbles between kisses "how wet are you baby?" His voice turned more deep than ever which turned me on more, I moan feeling him press his hard erection against me "yeah, you feel that?" he whisper he presses himself more and back off I frown and look at him "thats how you make me feel" he says

He took us upstairs in out room and sat on the bed while I was still standing there all hot "Come on I want your hands on my cock"

I bit my lip walking closer sitting on my knee I kept my hand on his thigh he watched my every move I unzipped his pants and brought them down following with his boxers

I cupped his manhood in my hand slowly moving my hand up and down I swirl my tongue around his tip "fuck" he whispered holding my hair from behind I slowly started sucking his cock bobbing my head up and down while his mouth fell open as his eyes closed and he looked incredibly sexy, he came after some minutes

He pulled my hand and I sat on his lap he captured my lips kissing me softly moving his lips with mine in sync, he slowly removed my dress leaving me in my bra and panties, his hands went on my back his cold ring hit my back making me shiver he unclipped the bra and removed it then his eyes went down to my chest he livked his bottom lips" you're so fucking beautiful baby"

His hands kneaded my breasts while my head thrown back as I moan loving his hands on me he pinched my nipple twisting it I bit my lip, his tongue swirled around my nipple and I gasped when he bit it gently sucking on it, his hands went down to my panties removing it his fingers felt my folds "soaking wet" he breathed in my ear nibbling it

His finger entered me, he slowly fingered me I gasped "faster please faster" I bit my lip, he entered three fingers, going faster this time I moaned loudly cumming after

He turned us around so now I was laying down He took out the small packet from drawer opening it with his teeth he wore it and settled himself between me I felt his tip making me crave him badly "Harry, please" I whimper

He chuckled sexily "no patience" I made eye contact with him giving him the look he smirked and kissed me

He was on top of me and he slowly entered me making both of us moan he started moving in and out faster after each thrust I held his shoulders as he thrust inside me my eyes rolled back and I moaned his name louder "thats right baby moan my name louder" he said

He looked so sexy some of his hair sticking to his forehead making him look ten times hotter his lip between his lips as he thrust inside me his eyes caught mine and he leaned down to kiss me his tongue collided with mine as he kissed me hard like he will be out of breathe if he stopped, his thumb circled on my clit I moan in his lips

(End of Mature Content)

After many rounds we finally stopped he dropped his forehead on mine breathing heavily he kissed me "I" he sucked my bottom lip "fucking" he bit my lip "love" his lips moved with mine "you" he said each word kissing me

We got up and took quick showers cleaning ourselves, I changed in my silk shorts and tank top while harry changed in his sweats

I laid down sighing closing my eyes, man I was exhausted

Bed dipped and harry shifted me closer to him so I was little spoon and he was big (cuddling) He kissed my cheek "did I hurt you?" He mumbled making me smile I turned around kissing his lips shaking my head he smiled back

I burried my face in his chest and his arms were around my waist

I loveeeeeee him

..

I felt sunlight hit my face I rubbed my eyes and blinked looking around, we forgot to close the drapes

Harry was sleeping peacefully with a small smile on his face, he looked so cute with messy hair covering his forehead I touched his lips pecking it softly

I carefully get up not waking him up I went to bathroom washing my face brushing my teeth tying my hair up in a bun,

I went closer to the bed softly calling his name to wake him up but he was sleeping soundly so I laid down aswell as the lazy ass I am..

I move closer to him and felt heat of his body, yes he was always warm but this was extra warn so I put the back of my hand on his forehead, my eyes widened as I felt how hot he wasOh god does he have a fever?

I cup one of his cheek and yes he is having a fever.. I push the strands of his hair that were on his forehead back "Baby" i whisper to him softly I shake him a little He hummed in response his eyes still closed

"Darling you're having a fever a bad fever" i say worried He opens his eyes a little and looked at me

He run his hands lazily on his hair "But I gotta go to work" his voice really deep than it is

I cupped his cheeks leaning in to capture his lips, I kiss him softly he smiled in the kiss, no matter he is sick or what I am still kissing him

I back off then I kissed him on forehead "You don't have to, I am gonna call the doctor okay?" I say softly caressing his cheek

He nodded "okay" his voice gruff, I pouted as I felt bad for my baby I hugged him and I heard him chuckle "you're gonna catch my fever" he says I lean a little back to look at his face and he had this sweet smile on his face "I don't care" I reply tilting my head

I covered him nicely with blanket and I went down to cook him breakfast, I cooked hot cocoa with simple eggs

I took the tray up to our room and he was still covered in blanket, I smiled and put the tray on the side table he slowly sit up his eyes were lazily opened

I sat beside him brushing his hair with my fingers kissing his forehead "I'll feed you okay? Don't worry" I say and he send me the cute smile

I feed him the eggs and hot cocoa, I brought medicine with it and he was being quite a baby not taking medicine

"Harry come on.. for me please?" I made puppy eyes and pouted he groaned "you always cheat" I smile and handed him the medicine he gulped it with a glass of water

I wiped his mouth with my thumb and took a tissue paper to clean his chin, yes he was eating like a baby

I was about to stand Keyword: about

He pulled my hand and I dropped on bed on top of him with a squealed "you're not going anywhere, you're staying here with me whole day and I am not taking no as an answer" he said hugging me tightly against him

Aww

I hugged him back and I laid beside him without saying anything as he pulled me incredibly close to him burying his face in my chest and sighing I play with his hair when I felt that he had fallen asleep

I smile seeing his face totally buried in my chest and I did not mind honestly, he needed to be treat like a baby now and I will treat him like one, I like to do it

I called the doctor and he checked in on harry and said he have gotten viral so it was normal and nothing to worry about he gave him some medicines which will make him feel better.

Harry was feeling alot better now than he was in the morning, he scrolled his phone while I was folding clothes "Oh Mr John uploaded the engagement pictures" harry said and my eyes widened my head snapped towards him "harry" I called he hummed "harry, look at me" I say he does

"Don't look at pictures you can meet Mrs John on their wedding day" I say, I know ! It was too obvious

He frown "wha-" I cut him off

"Just don't" I say

He sighed and tilted his head slightly "what is it?" He asked I shook my head "nothing"

He looked at me for some time then his eyes went back to his phone, his face went blank

"Harry?" I say.. he stayed quiet just looking at the picture

Then he frowned concentrating on the phone

"Harry what is it?" I ask again

He dropped his phone aside closing his eyes and taking a deep breathe

He turned towards me "you knew it was my mom right?" He asked as his eyes were filled with anger

I blinked at him not knowing what to say

This is gonna be long night..

....

Hii!! I am so sorry for the cliff hanger! But the chapter will be up soon so you will not have to wait long

Tell me about how do you like the story so far? I would love to hear from you guys!

Part 35

A lexa

Harry was mad

And really really mad

"I am asking something Alexa" he said with gritted teeth his voice filled with rage as his eyes burned with anger, I release a shaky breath then nodding my head slowly

"You fucking knew!?" His voice suddenly raised as he got up from bed

"I- yes I k-knew but I-"

"You know how much I am fucking affected with this situation" his brows furrowed deeply and I couldn't make eye contact with him

"Harry hear me out-"

"No! I don't want to fucking hear any Fucking thing, do you hear me?" His voice low and deadly

I took a step towards him hesitantly he raised his hand "stay right where you are don't come fucking close to me" he warned

I still took one more step "I SAID STAY FUCKING AWAY!" He yelled and I flinched scared by him

I quickly back out gulping

He pinched the bridge of his nose tapping his foot "get out" he muttered

I frowned lightly "what?"

"Get out" he say clearly

"Harry you're mistaken I am not at no one' side.. Please listen to me-"

"Get.out" his teeth gritted as he said it one more time

a tear escaped my eyes as I saw him not looking me in the eye he turned his back on me and a sob escaped my mouth I know he heard it he did, but he didn't turned around

I slowly made my way towards the door but he calls my name so I stopped not turning around just standing where I am holding the door knob

"I don't want to see your face so don't come infront of me whenever I am home, your room will be 3 doors away from my room" he said quietly looking out of the window

I looked at him one more time tried saying something but I gulped the words I nodded "okay" saying softly

..

I was cooking dinner when one of the maid came "Ma'am, Sir called he'll be late so he wouldn't be able to make it to dinner"

I know he is doing it on purpose he said he don't wanna see me so here it is this is how he's dealing with it

I smiled slightly nodding to the maid

I ate the dinner in silence and washed the dishes then went up to my room changing in my nightsuit when the door bell ranged

It must be harry... I couldn't open it he said he doesn't wanna see me so what I should wear a mask? what in the world

I slowly go downstairs gulping I open the door and shocked to see George standing there

"george?" I say confused to see him here with a smile on his face

"Hi there old bestie, what is up?" He asked grinning

I chuckle awkwardly "great.. uh what about you?"

"Well you know all same" he shrugged

"Is harry home?" He asked looking around

I shook my head "no he'll be late"

"aren't you gonna invite me in?" He raise his eyebrows

Harry said he never wanted me alone with george but he isn't talking to me right now and besides george looks fine

"Ofcourse come in" I smile

He came in while I closed the door "would you like to have anything?" I turn around smiling

"Yes..." he smiled, I tilted my head slightly

which faded away

"Revenge" he said

I was starting to panic when I chuckle nervously "wha- what? You must be joking right? This is the weirdest joke george"

His eyes glared at me as he move towards me I back off shaking my head "no george"

He smirked that dirty smirk

"What'd you think? I would just go away like that? Huh??" He asked loudly

A sweat trickle down my neck as I shook my head "I- I didn't do anything to you george"

He strided towards me gripping my hair tightly I screamed it felt like it will fall out "You fucking Bitch" he said and then laughed I frowned at him wincing when he tighten his hold "don't worry honey" he caressed my cheek which I removed his hand "i'll kill you before you know it" he grinned

I kicked him where sun doesn't shine and he screamed "You Whore!!" He fall down holding it

I ran upstairs how fast I could but he was fast and he catch me halfway through the stairs and he slapped me hard across the face making me wince he slapped me again more harder this time I whimper with pain He punched me in the face making me fall down on the stairs my mouth and nose started to bleed he kneed me in the stomach too many times I blink slowly taking slow breaths everything was turning blurry

"g-george p-please" I mumbled holding my stomach

He bend down "oh now you're begging??" He chuckled then kicked me harder and I fall down the stairs and I fall in darkness

Harry

I sighed as I leaned back on my chair

Something was odd something wasn't right my gut feeling is telling me that something happened

Weird thoughts came to my mind as I think about Alexa

I quickly grabbed my car keys and stepped out of my office leaving right away I got in my car speeding from the streets in some minutes I reached home parking the car I stepped out of it locking it

I walked closer to the door and stopped the door was opened and wide opened, An alarm went off in the back of my head telling me there is nothing right

I slowly walked inside and looked around my eyes alarmed as I looked everywhere I started to walk in slowly and stopped dead in my tracks when I saw alexa on the fucking ground with blood all over her

I lost my senses when I ran to her kneeling down My eyes widened as they start to well up, I held her face in my hands carefully, caressing it "A-alexa" my voice uneven

"No no no no no no NO ALEXA! Please p-please wake up A-Alexa look at me" tears started coming down my eyes uncontrollably I shake her slightly I hugged her tightly close to me Screaming

"Please don't leave me, p-please I am sorry I am so fucking sorry" I sob in her chest as I hold her close to me

"Please.. I- I b-beg you Alexa" my voice breaking as I try to wake her up

I scooped her in my arms as her blood covered all over my suit I remove my jacket covering her body I lay her carefully on the passenger seat I get in driver seat driving as fast as I can while tears coming down my face, every now and then I look at her but she stay still not moving

After reaching the nearest hospital I carry her bridal style and ran in hospital shouting to help Many doctors surround me while laying Alexa down and taking her to emergency room

I held her hand tightly "you'll be fine you'll be fine" I murmured to her

Her face pale and covered with marks and blood

"Sir please wait here we'll inform you" The nurse said

"THAT'S MY FUCKING WIFE!, IF SOMETHING..ANYTHING HAPPENED TO HER I WILL BURN DOWN THIS HOSPITAL WITH YOU ALL IN IT" I yell at everyone

The nurse rushed inside the room

I paced back and forth checking the time it was more than 4 hours and doctor wasn't out

I sit down laying my head back closing my eyes I started sobbing shaking lightly as I hold my face in my hands

Its all my fault all my fucking fault I left her alone, Why did that happened to her?? It should've been me!

I called every person I knew for finding out who was the one that left my house last time

I swear who ever it is I will make them die the worst slow and painful death that's my promise to Alexa and myself

My phone rang as I picked it up holding it to my ears not saying anything
"Sir we saw who it is"

I froze my jaw clenching hard "who?"

I'll forward you the picture we found on the camera he send me the photo
I opened it and I felt I turned red

My knuckles turned white for how hard I fist it my jaw clenched my nose
flared as I glared at the picture burning holes in it

"Okay. Whats his current location tell me each and every fucking thing"

"Yes sir right away" he say

I ended the call laying back

George

That motherfucker doesn't know what he get himself into

"Excuse me sir?" Doctor called me I turned towards him

"Yes? What is it? Is she fine?" i ask hurriedly

"Yes she is fine" he said I release a breath I don't know I was holding "you
can see her she's awake and I have to tell you both a news" he said I frowned

I walked in opening the door seeing her laying down her eyes closed

I sat beside her holding her hand her eyes shot open as she turn towards me

Tears build up in my eyes as I stare at her I cupped her cheeks "Oh my god"
I whisperShe held my hand "harry" her voice hoarse

"Baby... I am so... so so so sorry I- I don't know what to say" I whisper
closing my eyes

"Its okay harry I am fine" she said slowly

"No you are not... I wasn't there.. You are my world.. what would I do without you.. please don't ever leave me" my voice breaking as I say so

With weak hands she cupped my cheek "no, I will never leave you...ever" she pressed her forehead with mine I breathe

"He beat me....bad" she whispered closing her eyes which were tightly closed

"I am going to kill him, I promise you" I say kissing her lips softly

Before she could say anything the doctor knocked the door I said come in and he did closing the door

"How are you feeling Alexa?" He asked

She nodded "okay"

"Okay.. You'll be discharged in 15 days. there is something" He say

Alexa frowned "what is it doctor?"

He takes a deep breath

"I am sorry to say but.... your baby its not breathing" he said

I frowned and Alexa looked shock utterly shocked "B-baby?" She chuckled nervously

He nodded "I am afraid he is no more because something hit your stomach and it caused danger to baby as well"

Alexa gasped "T-there was a baby?" She whispered

"You didn't knew?"

She shook her head

"He was of 4 weeks"

My heart broke

She release a harsh breathe "I am sorry what?" She asked not sinking in

I held her hand tightly as I nodded to doctor he left

I caressed her back as she look at the ceiling "4 weeks." She repeated slowly

I take a harsh breathe nodding "yes"

She looked at me "we were gonna have a baby.. I was pregnant" she whispered as her voice broke

I can not take this much

I caressed her cheek nodding not knowingHow to console her

"W-what what did the baby did wrong to him?" She asked me tilting her head as tears drop from her eyes I wipe them away

She take a breath and broke down crying loudly I hugged her tightly towards me she buried her face in my chest sobbing loudly as I caress her back and her hair kissing her head

"My baby.....died" she sobbed looking at me her face was red so was her eye "harry our baby died, it died because of him! Because of him!" She yelled hugging me tightly hiccuping "please t-tell me i-its all a nightmare" she mumbled

I wish it was

I hugged her tightly and she cried her heart out

My eyes burned with anger as I stared at the wall when she sobbed in my arms

George... Just wait

I am coming for you......

"Sir as you said we've kidnapped him he's now in the basement locked" one of my workers informed me

"I am gonna be there, keep an eye on him" I say

....

This was the most heartbreaking chapter I had to write! They didn't deserved it!! At allPlease comment how was the chapter!?

I Love Y'all

Part 36

HAPPY NEW YEAR Y'ALL LET'S HOPE THIS YEAR BRINGS ENDLESS JOYS IN YOUR LIFE! This chapter is for you ;)

Harry

All I could see was red this time when I was leaving for the house

I left grandma at the hospital to look after alexa who was crying non stop her eyes were red from how much she have cried

My anger was building up every second I get closer to the house

I stepped out of the car reloading my gun and tugging it in my back pocket I walked straight towards the basement

There was an abandon room where he was tied up, I opened the door and saw him sitting on a chair his face duck taped his hands and legs tied with a rope

his eyes were closed as his face was low

All I wanted to do was put the fucking bullet through his head but I am gonna make his death slow and painful

Torture in further chapter If you're not comfortable you can skip the c hapter☐

My eyes deadly focused on him as I took my gun out and walked towards him, a low light hanging above the ceiling I sat across him hitting his forehead with the back of gun lightly to wake him up

His eyes opened as he looked towards me blinking a few times then his eyes went wide as he came to his senses I smirked evilly seeing how afraid he was

"Hm, so where should we start from" I rub my forehead releasing a breathe "huh george?" My jaw clenched hard as I glare at him

His eyes terrified as he saw a gun in my hand I followed his eyes and looked at the gun scoffing "oh this is nothing" I got up walking towards him bending down face to face "for what I've planned for you" I say in low voice my voice filled with venom

His voice muffled as he tried to say something I took the end of the tape opening it he hissed a little sighing "I-I am s-s-sorry"

I looked at him emotionless without saying anything "you're what?"

"I said I- am s-sor-" before he could finish I took the knife and sliced the corner of his mouth he screamed from the pain as his mouth started bleeding

I held his jaw tightly with my hand nearly crushing it for how tight the grip was "Oh how its sounds music to my ear" I said through gritted teeth removing my hand from there with a pressure

I untied his hands and he looked at me confused I brought the knife towards his hand and opened his fingers wide, looking at his eyes I say "you better keep them wide opened" warning him his eyes widened

I looked deadly in his eyes and started moving the knife from one finger to another he saw his hand and screamed "no no no please!" I smirked and closed my eyes then I stabbed his hand and opened my eyes as he screamed I pushed the knife more inside tears fall from his eyes "I am sorry!!" He said I tilt my head "oh now you are begging?" throwing his words at him he seemed shocked by that

I removed the knife and he screamed more

I sighed and took the bigger knife putting it on his shoulder I looked at him "we should start with this hand right?" He shivered with terror I removed it and put it on his other shoulder "or... this one?"

He doesn't answer and just shivered I backed off and call one of the man he came bowing "yes sir"

I sat down on chair putting my leg on other "would you do the honours?" I ask as I nodded towards george he looked at george and nodded right away "sure sir"

I smirked "good, start then" I lay back on my seat lighting my cigarette inhaling the smoke watching the show as he walked towards george and cut all of his fingers one by one I saw him beg and beg and beg

Anger build up in me for thinking of my baby I stood up striding towards him and pushed the man away he was shocked but then bowed siding away I grabbed his jaw as my nose flared he was unconscious as his eyes were almost closed "What the fuck did my baby do? Hm?" I tilted my head he couldn't answer so I yelled "YOU FUCKING KILLED MY BABY!" I took the gun out and lost all my cools as I shot him on the forehead the chair fall down I shot him again and again and again until the bullets ended

A tear fall from my eyes as I stare at his dead body I wiped it away walking out "clean the mess" I told the man he nodded

I walked away from the house and looked up at the sky my chest rose and fell from every harsh breath I take

I lit the cigarette and put it in my mouth as the smoke release from the corner of my mouthI run a hand on my hair looking around my eyes started to well up as I looked up at the sky again with blurry eyes

Men cries too...

This time was really hard for Alexa and me losing a child isn't easy and how it is I feel it and it is shittiest feeling a person could go through.. Alexa was fucking pregnant and I couldn't have been more happier I was gonna be a fucking father... but we lost our baby and I blame myself for all of it

....

Part 37

A lexa

(4 months later)

These last few months were really hard for me I never talked alot as I used to I usually stayed quiet but harry was there every single time he was there for me whenever I was angry sad or whatsoever he never pushed me back instead he embrace me in his arms

I have been alot better than I was, I've started to act all normal and not think about it that much because, that shit hurts badly

Today was the day harry thought of talking to his mother and I was really happy for what he decided, Mr John was married and technically now Mr John was harry's step father

Harry left in the morning to meet her.. I have decided to visit the cafe I used to work in It fees like its been a decade since I worked there

I got off from the car walking towards the cafe all the memories filled me... the worst part was george and only him Well jack also

I walked inside the cafe as I see new faces there the interior was a little changed and it was more advanced

I walked to the counter and saw a beautiful blonde "Hi Ma'am what can I get for you?" Her face light up as she asks nicely

I smile "can I meet the manager?" Her face filled with worry I quickly shook my head "no you didn't do anything wrong, Actually I used to work here so the manager was a nice friend of mine" I explain totally lying about the friend thing, nice friend my ass.. she nods sighing with relief after she heard what was I saying

She walks inside the staff room and I saw jack come out he looked older and his hair were grey he wore his casual clothes as he had notepad in his hands following with a pen, he looked around and his eyes landed on me and He was shocked to the core as he saw me "Alexa" he say quietly

"Jack" I fake smiled but it looked real walking towards him shaking his hand "how's everything been?" I look around, though some bad memories also filled me where he used to beat me but lets just leave it in the past I mean he is a nice guy now

I don't even know!!Well just wait

"great actually we have many customers daily and everything's been great well lets just leave this tell me about you how have you been?" He asked seeming interested, never seemed that interested in my life when I use to work here short dick I nearly scoffed but stopped myself

I pass a small smile "Good" I do not tell him further as he nods understand-ing I won't tell him my private things to him I would rather let a tiger eat me alive than to share my problems and secrets with Jack

"Well where is the scary Large gorilla man" he laughs making a pathetic joke and pushing the button he shouldn't have I narrow my eyes at him telling him clearly I didn't liked the joke his smile vanished

"He isn't a" I mimic his voice weirdly "ScArY LaRgE GoRiLlA" I click my tongue "only I am aloud to call him that you listen here mister" I point my finger at him he seemed shocked

He tried to glare but I stopped him by saying "Oh don't you dare try to do that glary thing with me cause my husband gonna sue your ass" I warn him "and buddy don't even think he will go easy with you" I chuckle stopping "cause he won't"

He actually looked scared "y-you can't blackmail me in m-my restaurant" he tired raising his voice

"Or what? Huh? Or what are you gonna do you short dick" I say suddenly everyone's eyes snapped at me shockingly all the staff customer looked at me

"What? You don't believe me? Okay fine look at it then" I point at his dick and everyone's eyes went down there

He covered that part "ay ay ay what the hell, everyone get back to your own business!" He said and people agreed

He turned towards me and narrowed his eyes "and I DO NOT have a short dick" he says loudly so everyone could hear

"Whatever donkey, I am gonna go not nice meeting you" I say rolling my eyes and turning around walking away then I stopped and turned back "And a little advice, stuck your face up the girl's ass maybe then she likes your short dick" I say feeling all badass as my eyes flick down there he quickly covered it confusingly looking at me I smirked

Haha sucker

I walked out and release a breathe I don't know I was holding, man that was hard! It was my dream goal to talk to him like that well I did thankfully

A wind blow through my hair as I walk down the street humming some song tapping on my phone My chest collided with someone making me almost fall back I gasped as I handled my balance

I narrowed my eyes and turned around fully ready to scream at the person but then all of the colours faded away from my face, my eyes couldn't believe who I saw in front of me the last person I wanted to see

My mother

I look at her not saying anything, she passed me a small smile stepping forward but I stopped her immediately shaking my head silently telling no

She sighed as she stop "Alexa" she say quietly, my ears used to love that voice sometime but I can't stand it now

"Mom, I-I am sorry I ca-" she cut me off

"I have cancer" she said

Silence

I stayed quiet only sinking in what the hell did she just say... I chuckle "mom this is the pathetic joke if you want me to come back because I won't" I say sternly she frowns "no sweety I am not lying... how could I prove it to you?" She says sweetly

"Your reportcards" I nodded she nodded right away "or your doctor" I added

"Whatever that will make you believe" she finishes then start walking I followed her texting harry

MeI'll be a little late, will tell you everything when I come home..

HusbandOkay be safe please..

I smile at his text

HusbandText me your location though

I roll my eyes texting a 'yes'

I followed mom and she took me to an apartment that looked really old the building was damaged I look around "you live here?" I ask

"Yes I could only afford this" she says and suddenly my heart aches badly

She opened her apartment door and we get inside "Please sit I'll bring something" she said and disappeared in kitchen

She came back holding a glass of juice I drank it thanking her then without wasting any time she showed me her reports and my heart drops because they were real!

I look at her through my eyelashes totally shocked "you h-have lung cancer?" I ask hesitantly, she nods slowly looking down

I quickly hugged her tightly crying "H-how did th-this happen?" I ask crying as my tears wet her shoulder

She caress my hair "When I called you it was because I needed your help I wanted money and not for my fun but for cancer treatment.. then I found a job somewhere near and I didn't called you after thinking of not bothering you, but sometime I needed to tell you so I bumped into you today" she finishes

I wipe my tears shaking my head "you could've called me again..." I sighed "I- I amgoing to help you through all this and you are going to come live with me.. Please" I insisted

She nods then smile "okay and thankyou-"

"No Mom.. please don't" I say then hugged her again

I will help her and pay for all her cancer treatment..

But I have to tell Harry..

Harry

Now that I have sorted things out with myMother she told me her side of story and I gave in... I asked her to come live with me to leave john and let me take care of her.. she said she'll think about it

And I have to tell Alexa...

.....

Okay!!!! The book is gonna finish soon enough!

Part 38 (second last)

A lexa

I take mom with me to home,I will talk to harry when he come back but now I just need to take her with me

"Mom this is your room, please make yourself comfortable I'll be upstairs if you need anything" I say as I show her room sheLooked stunned looking around

"Thankyou honey" she whispers then she looks at me for some minutes her eyes shining "I- I don't know what to say" she wipes her tear and look away

I walk towards her hugging her "its okay mom, I forgive you its alright forget the past please" I whispers sweetly she nods slowly sighing and backing off "I'll go freshen up" she smiles slightly I pass it back, exiting her room I took my phone and called harry

Ringing....

"Hey"

"Hi" I smile, just by hearing his voice a smile makes it way to my face "uhh When will you come back?" I ask

"I am on my way, I need to talk to you about something" he says

"Oh, well" I chuckle "same...goes for me" biting my lip I tell him

"Okay, I'll be there in 5" I hear some women's voice behind but ignoring it I say

"Cool see you buddy"

"Don't you dare-"

I decline the call, laughing lightly shaking my head.. he hates when I call him bro buddy or something that means 'brother' and I love to tease him

I get inside the bathtub soaking inside and sighing leaning my head closing my eyes I think about every thing thats happening lately in my life, it is just up and down and I've been in a freaking roller coaster just seeing what the hell is happening in my lifeLoosing a baby made me so hollow that I stopped talking my world turned upside down.. I used to have nightmares thankfully harry by myside I used to be okay

(A lil bit mature)

I hear door opening and closing.. he's here

"I am in here" I say so he could know

I hear his footsteps coming here I sit up looking at the door as he opened it and came inside

His hair was messy and hot as ever some of the strands sticking to forehead, his suit jacket was off as well as his tie, his arm flexed as he take off his shirt unbuttoning it and throwing it aside, he removed his pants leaving him in boxers

He smirked at me and tilted his head "what we have planned here?" His deep voice filled the bathroom

I bit my lip chuckling "nothing for you"

He cocked an eyebrow smirk still there "oh really?"

"Mhm" I dip my fingers in the water swirling it

His tongue touched the inside of his cheek as he say "do you think i'll just turn around and leave baby?" he takes step towards the tub

I gulp and smile at him shaking my head

His finger grabbed my chin lifting it up so ai could meet his eyes "what did you called me before?" He asks his grey eyes scanning my eyes

"Nothing" I fight the urge to smile

He hums, he lean down and kissed my neck a featherlight kiss making me want more I grabbed the back of his neck as he sucked my soft spot making me moan a little

"What did you said baby?" He asks whispering in my neck

I pant "daddy" I said that word because I listened somewhere guys like it when you call them addressing this, At first I found it weird but now I am enjoying the look he's giving me

I felt him froze as he lifts his head up looking me in the eye he look back and forth through right and left eye "say it again"

I lick my lips "daddy" I say

I hear him growl as he catches my mouth in his kissing me hungrily like he wants to tell me how much he loves doing that, that he can't breathe without it We back off and he pressed his forehead with mine "Fuck, lex you make me wanna fuck you so hard you couldn't walk for weeks" he nuzzle his nose with mine then kissing it

(end of mature content)

Me and harry showered and cleaned up as we walk downstairs

I take harry to mom's bedroom, I knock on the door as me and harry waits patientlyI knock again but didn't hear anything, I look at harry and his eyes were concerned "open it" he whisper I turn around and twist the knob slowly opening the door I saw mom laying on the bed her eyes closed and mouth opened a bit

I quickly hurried to her side, I shake her a little "mom" I say softly she doesn't respond

"Mom harry is here" shaking her a little I say she doesn't move I look at harry worriedly as my eyes started to fill with tears he grabs my hand squeezing it "I'll call the ambulance" he disappeared outside I grabbed mom's hand rubbing it a little to keep her warm she was cold I shiver a little thinking of bad things

Ambulance arrived in some time we took her to the hospital

"She isn't waking up" I breathe telling to doctor

"Miss, we need to see what is going on.. I'llInform you about the condition" the doctor said and went inside emergency room

I sat down on the chair rocking my feet fiddling with my fingers as I wait patiently

Harry went to bring his mother.. I was happy and shocked to know he was now okay with his mother.. I will ask him about what exactly happened

I bury my face in my hands sighing as I think of worst things to happen that makes me scared to death

I felt someone put a hand on my shoulder I look up and saw harry with his mother she was smiling sadly at me

I got up and hugged her tightly "oh honey she'll be okay.." she says

A sob escaped my mouth "I-I don't know" She caress my back kissing my head saying nice words to me

.

She went to washroom as me and harry sat waiting for mom

Harry grabbed my hand so I stand up then he pulled me down to his lap and god it was so comfy as he was wearing sweatpantsI bury my face in his chest he kisses my forehead constantly intertwining his fingers with mine

"Will she be okay?" I mumble to him he caress my hair kissing it "ofcourse she will baby" he says softly

"I am a-afraid" I close my eyes tightly inhaling his scent which was com-forting for my mind

He cupped my cheeks wiping tears away with his thumb he pressed his forehead with mine "you never need to be afraid of anything when I am here with you, always" he whisper kissing my lips softly, then pulling me more close to him, I laid my head on his shoulder as he comforts me saying sweet things

..

I didn't know when I nodded off but I jerked when someone under me moved

I look up to see who it is rubbing my eye

A large hand quickly comes behind my head as he gently pushes me in his chest "shh sleep.. sorry" he whispers softly

I sigh as I closed my eyes hearing his heartbeat... the only thing thats keeping me alive

I lay my cheek on his chest "I am awake" I mumble

"I am sorry baby, I just wanted you to get more comfortable" He say slowly, laying his cheek on my head rubbing my arm to keep me warm as it was a bit cold

I smile slightly kissing his cheek "I am okay, and I slept well"

He hums in response sweetly as I nod my head

"Anything about mom?" I ask tracing his shirt with my finger

He shake his head "the doctor haven't come out yet"

"Where's your mom?" I lean back to look at him he looks down at me, those beautiful eyes filled with adoring and loving feeling

"She went home" he replied quietly

"Oh" I say looking around there was no one in this area

I turn towards harry who was already looking at me with a tiny smile on his face

"Harry?"

"Love?" He grabs my hand inter-wining it and caressing my knuckles

"Tell me what happened when you went to meet your mother?" I ask my eyes scanning his eyes

He nods..

- Harry's POV (FLASHBACK)

I park my car getting of it fixing my shirt as I make my way inside some cafe she called me to meet

My eyes search around as it caught the familiar ones staring right back at me

I approach where she was seated slowly not showing any kind of emotion

"Mother" I said sternly looking at her

She passed me small smile "harry, thankyou for time-" I cut her off

"Can we skip this?" I raise an eyebrow

She sighed "sure" she gestured to the seat "please"

I blinked and sat down sitting straight inter-wining my fingers together keeping them on the table "talk" I say

She took a deep breathe and started

Third person's POV (Back when Harry was kid)

Harry's mother made amazing lunch for her son and her husband as she was really happy today, grateful for everything she has

Mr.Stewart was in his office room working currently and harry was in school right now

She wiped her hands with a cloth a small smile playing on her face as she hums a random song

She made her way towards where his office was, without knocking she slowly twisted the knob and her smile dropped immediately when she saw that

A small gasp escape from her mouth she quickly covered it with her trembling hands

Harry's father was kissing his secretary Claire that was on his lap he seem to enjoy it alot as he grabbed her ass tightly

Her vision become blurry as she closed the door slowly walking out utterly shocked for what she saw

She walk in kitchen with empty mind she look at the dishes she made

She felt a small voice call her "mama!"

She turn around seeing harry approach her with a paper in his hand she quickly wipe her tears away as harry showed his report card to his mother seeing she was sad he felt sad too but her mother quickly covered it up

Next day she decided to leave this place along with harry forever and never return

She sigh as she walk where harry was asking him to come with her Telling him that they are going to someone's house he shook his head with a small frown clearly telling he didn't liked the idea

Her eyes caught that harry's father was staring at her with some doubt in his eyes

She smiled at harry and walked towards her husband, betrayal was all she felt when she looked at him

"Harry will not go with you" he said sternly

"But-"

"I said No" his eyes dangerously glaring at her

She seem to have no way but to leave alone for now

She quickly big goodbye to harry and made her way somewhere

The driver looked at her with a knowing look

She offered driver enough money to help her

A bomb was planted in this car and harry'sMother and driver jumped out of the car before it was about to cross the bridge

saving their lives they saw car explode infront of them

They put false bodies there with their faces completely ruined so no one could find out

After that day she daily made some plan to go get harry but harry's father strict the safety Cameras surrounded all of the house

Then one day they shifted away, and she didn't knew where she tried to ask neighbours but no one knew

There was no way now

She used to look at harry's picture and cry everyday to sleep for one day she will meet him

After many years she saw news of his son famous businessman tears of happiness filled her eyes as she saw him achieve what he wanted to be

She found out that Mr John was harry's closest partner and she somehow made him fall in love with her

What she did was wrong but no idea came to her brain as she only thought about meeting him seeing him

(End of mother's story)

Tears continuously fall from my eyes as I stare at my mother with alot of emotions

How could I not trust my mother?How? Why?

Hi couldn't hold back as I got up from my seat kneeling down and hugging her

I heard mom sob quietly "you don't know how much I've waited for you to just hug me look me how you used to do when you were small" she whisper

I back off wiping her tears away "I am so..so sorry Mama I-" I hugged her again

I could feel happiness, sadness everything

His jaw clenched hard as he thought of his father that motherfucker

Claire was his fucking secretaryHow come I never knew

That bastard will pay for this he will fucking pay for every tear my mother have cried

- (FLASHBACK ENDED)

Alexa

A tear escaped his eye as he looked at me without any emotion

I grabbed his head and buried his face in my chest wanting him closer "oh god" I whisper

He sighed hugging me more close to him

I hear a door opened I turn slightly aroundTo see doctor come out

He took off his mask about to tell how my mother is

I took a deep breathe as I wait for his answer

.....

Second last part!! I cannot believe □□

How was the whole story?? Please do Vote And comment!

Part 39

~ Epilogue is included in this chapter~

-

Alexa

I was looking at the doctor waiting for him to speak

He sigh and looked at harry shaking his head

He stilled as the doctor went away putting a hand on my shoulder with a sorry face

I frown looking at him totally confused why is he acting this way

I turn towards harry who was also looking at me with same feelings in his eyes that doctor looked at me

I get off his lap standing up "what is it?" I ask

"your mother...she" he inhale through his mouth holding a breathe for a second then letting go "she is no more"

I stand there

why?

Staring at him without any thoughts coming to my mind As if My brain stopped working and I was staring at nowhere

Voice of different people filled my ears

Some of them crying for the lost of a loved one while some of them thanking god to save the ones they were praying for

A little shake bring me back and I looked up at him

His eyes were filled with worry as he hug me tightly I stare at the floor not saying anything nor hugging him back

He don't understand He will never How it fucking feels right now

..

"I am so sorry" someone said to me as I say nothing

I've heard their sorries million times every person right here just say this one thing and go away as if this sorry will bring her back as if this sorry will make everything right

"You haven't eaten anything" I hear him say as he come sit beside me and I look nowhere

"I am not hungry"

Silence

He sighs "please eat something" he whisper softly putting his hand on my knee

I move his hand away shaking my head

-Harry

She was so empty

I could never imagine the pain she must be feeling

She haven't cried her heart out like she do She is too tired

I wish I could take all of her pain away from her Why can't I do that?

Somehow I make her eat little bit after that she went to our room not saying anything to anyone

I make my way upstairs and warned every one of them to not follow me or come upstairs

I walk inside the room and she was there sitting on bed her head tilted and she was looking down

My heart breaks completely seeing her like this

I slowly make my where she was sitting

"Why do they always leave?" I hear her quiet voice

"Sometimes its for the best"

She falls back on bed "I wanna sleep harry please take this pain away from me, this headache, this ache in the heart take it away please" she whispers her voice breaking

I take her hand making her sit I kiss her forehead softly "give me all of it, all of your pain everything give it to me, take the burden of your heart"

She sighs and close her eyes "hold me close"

I carefully take her in my arms and lay down on bed without leaving her, I hold her close to me so her head leans on my chest

I caress her hair "Sleep my love..I am here for you, I am never leaving"

Soon I hear her breaths even as she fell asleep in my arms

.Alexa

Its been few months and I've been better

I started seeing some therapist as I was too mentally disturbed I've started to move on from her death and trying to accept it

Harry have been taking me to endless places trying to divert my mind he is always trying to make me smile or laugh and is always successful

"My sugar I brought you some flowers" he gave me a bouquet of white tulips

A smile find its way on my face as he gives it to me

Also about the nickname he has been calling me different names and I enjoy it

He pecks my lips "so where do you wanna go? What about umm" he taps his finger on his chin thinking cutely as a strand of his hair fall on his forehead

I bite my lip to hide the smile as I shrug

"What about the.....bedroom?" He asks smirking

I giggle "hmm, I don't know" I tease him as a he frowns cutely

I grin shuffling his hair "I am kidding my donut" I nuzzle my nose with him

He smiles and winks "lead the way then"

I smirk and turn around swaying my hips from every step I take I know he's drooling by now

We walk inside the bedroom

As he sits down on bed gesturing towards the door "don't want mom to hear you scream now do we?" He smirks naughtily

A gasp escape my lips and my cheeks turn pink

He loose his tie and his eyes turned dark "Now" he commands and I was almost on my knees

I know very well what he was referring to sl I walk towards the door looking at my shoulder at him then at the door

I lick my lips biting it

I am ready, always

- Door Closed-

————

Epilogue

"So why are we inviting so many people on dinner?" He asks me "I mean it can be only few"

And I roll my eyes huffing

He have asked me this question a million times by now because we have never invited so many people at our house but its a big day!

"Honey, Its a big day, I want everyone to join us" I kiss his cheeks as a frown was set on his face permanently

I shake my head and head towards the walk in closet choosing my outfit

I choose a long dress olive green which is off shoulders and have a long slit starting from my upper thigh to the end which shows my long legs, sorry short legs whatever

"You should be better dressed up harry when I come out or else I'll kick you where the sun doesn't shine" I warn him

He chuckles "sun doesn't shine? What but You like that-"

"Harry!"

I hear him laugh and the warmth settle in my stomach as I hear his voice

I started getting ready doing little bit of makeup and changing in my ootn (outfit of the night)

I spray some cologne of harry because he have the best colognes and I love men's perfume so

I walk out of the closet in the room and saw harry brushing his hair looking in the mirror

He was looking drop dead gorgeous person

He was wearing a grey button down shirt following with pants his suit-jacket was on the chair beside him

I walk towards him and we make eye contact through mirror

"Whats up my sexy husband?" I ask smiling

He smirks and winks

I take the suitjacket and help him wear it

I dust off his shoulder keeping my hands there "perfect" I whisper

He leans down and kiss my lips softly sucking my lips and backing off he leans his forehead with mine "I love you"

"I love you" I say kissing his lips again and again he grins

We walk down the stairs hand in hand as I see there were many peopleHarry sure did invited most of the people he knew

We meet everyone and greet them

I excuse myself towards the bar I take a glass and take a spoon softly hitting it with my glass for everyone's attention

They all turn towards me and I make eye contact with harry his eyes soften

"Welcome everyone, thankyou for joining us today as it is really big day for us" I look at harry "our babygirl selena have turned 1 today" they all cheer "she's sleeping now though so please keep it down as its a really hard thing to put her to sleep" I chuckle and hear everyone chuckle with me harry smile

"Harry and I have faced many things together.... We lost our first baby" I stopped taking a few breaths as harry quickly come towards me putting his hand on my waist softly caressing it to calm me down in some way

I looked at harry "but we didn't give up.. We never left each other for anything and then I was pregnant" I smile as I look his eyes shine "it was unexplainable feeling that was rushing towards us when we held our babygirl in our hands for the first time, she brings life in this home All of our sorrow go away when we see her smile or giggle she's our little princess our joy... our selena" I finish as I hear applause, harry leans in and kiss me then kissing my forehead

Someone taps my shoulder I turn around and saw housekeeper Nancy "Selena is awake" she says and I nod smiling

I walk towards her room I open the door and see her sitting in her cot playing with her toy she looks so cute as she is wearing pink frock her chubby cheeks bounce as she mumble some things her hair come down to her forehead

"Hey baby" I say sweetly

She looks up at me and give me big smile a little tooth showing as she smile which flutter my heart

I walk towards her cot lifting her up in my arms as her small hands wrap around my finger I kiss her cheek and she lay her head on my shoulder

I can't take this much joy

I was about to walk out when I see harry come in he look at selena and smile "my princess, how are you?" He asks

She calls harry with her hand cutely and harry takes her in his arm

Harry kiss her cheek over and over again

"Can you say dada? Da da" he says

She giggles and try to say but mutter something else making me and harry chuckle

"Da da" he says again

"Harry she won't say it she is just 1-"

"Dada" she says her cute little voice filled the room as she say it

Harry grins "thats my baby!" He hugs her close to him and dances

I laugh

Harry turn towards me and selena too "you see Mama she is so gorgeous, yes thats right she is, and she is a queen she is a beautiful queen" he tells her as she turn towards harry looking at him slightly tilting her head

"Thats right, she is a queen and you are a princess"

I smile and walk towards them kissing harry's lips as we hear selena scream slightly

We turn towards her and she hug harry close to her telling me 'back off dada is mine'

I giggle "hey you, he is my man" I narrow my eyes at her playfully

She hugs him closer clearly saying no

Me and harry laugh looking at her

I love how my life turned

I love every person every moment of this life

I wish everything stay this way

I love both of them more than anything and I continue to do so.. as they are my whole world

.....